Pelican Books
PO: Beyond Yes & No

Edward de Bono was born in Malta and after his initial education at St Edward's College, Malta, and the Royal University of Malta, where he obtained a degree in medicine, he proceeded as a Rhodes Scholar to Christ Church, Oxford, where he gained an honours degree in psychology and physiology and then a D.Phil. in medicine. He also holds a Ph.D. from Cambridge. He has had faculty appointments at the universities of Oxford, London, Cambridge and Harvard.

Dr de Bono is the founder and director of the Cognitive Research Trust in Cambridge (founded 1969) and the Centre for the Study of Thinking. He runs what is now the largest curriculum programme in the world for the direct teaching of thinking in schools. Dr de Bono's instruction in thinking has been sought by many of the leading corporations such as IBM, Shell, Unilever, ICI, Du Pont and many others. He has been invited to lecture extensively throughout the world.

He has written many books which have been translated into nineteen languages. He has also completed two TV series, 'The Greatest Thinkers' for WDR, Germany, and 'De Bono's Course in Thinking' ... the originator of the term 'l... the classic L-game which ... invented.

Among ... ral Thinking (1967), The F... Mechanism of Mind (1969), ... -Exercising Machine (1970), Technology Today (1971), Practical Thinking (1971), Lateral Thinking for Management (1971), Children Solve Problems (1972), Eureka: an illustrated history of inventions from the wheel to the computer (1974), Teaching Thinking (1976), The Greatest Thinkers (1976), Wordpower (1977), The Happiness Purpose (1977), Opportunities: a handbook of business opportunity search (1978), Future Positive (1979), Atlas of Management Thinking (1981), De Bono's Course in Thinking (1982), Tactics: The Art and Science of Success (1985), Conflicts: A Better Way To Resolve Them (1985) and Six Thinking Hats (1986). Many of these have been published in Penguins. Dr de Bono has also contributed to many journals, including The Lancet and Clinical Science. He is married and has two sons.

Edward de Bono

PO
Beyond Yes & No

Penguin Books

Penguin Books Ltd, Harmondsworth, Middlesex, England
Viking Penguin Inc., 40 West 23rd Street, New York, New York 10010, U.S.A.
Penguin Books Australia Ltd, Ringwood, Victoria, Australia
Penguin Books Canada Limited, 2801 John Street, Markham, Ontario, Canada L3R 1B4
Penguin Books (N.Z.) Ltd, 182–190 Wairau Road, Auckland 10, New Zealand

First published by Simon and Schuster, New York 1972
This revised edition published in Pelican Books 1973
Reprinted 1974, 1975, 1976, 1977, 1978, 1980, 1983, 1984, 1986

Printed and bound in Great Britain by
Cox & Wyman Ltd, Reading
Set in Linotype Juliana

Contents

CONTENTS

CREATIVE PO

GENERAL PO

PRACTICAL PO

PO EXPERIMENT

PO PRACTICE

Preface to the Pelican Edition

This book was first published in the United States and that is why the style is perhaps more crisp and forthright than might otherwise have been the case. Some readers might be upset by this and might feel that a more gently persuasive manner with much qualification and scholarly reference would be more suitable for such a fundamental subject. They may be right, and I did consider completely re-writing the book in that way, rather than making only the adaptations necessary for the English reader, but in the end decided that if something was worth saying it was worth saying in as direct and simple a manner as possible. In any case the notion of PO is likely to upset many people however it is presented. If it did not have this effect it would probably not be worth presenting.

Those readers who are already familiar with my work on the treatment of thinking as a skill and also on lateral thinking will already have a natural framework into which to fit the book. They will find that PO crystallizes the amorphous attitudes and particular processes of lateral thinking into a symbol that can be used directly as a tool. Those readers who have not yet read any of my other books will find that PO can stand on its own, but they may want to read between the lines to find out what lies behind the starkness of PO.

Our traditional YES/NO thinking system is immensely effective in the second stage of thinking: that is in making the best use of fixed ideas. Unfortunately the system is not much use in the first stage of thinking: that is the perception stage which involves creating new ideas and new ways of looking at things.

PREFACE TO THE PELICAN EDITION

Just as NO is the basic tool of logical thinking so a new word PO is suggested as the basic tool for the first stage of thinking. Logical YES/NO thinking is based on *judgement* but PO thinking is based on *movement*. Both types of thinking are necessary. But we must realize that logic is unlikely to solve those problems which need a new idea for their solution. Today the world is rather full of such problems.

PO: Magic and Maths

The New Word PO

the new word

PO is a new word. If this word existed in language, only two other words would be more important. In twenty years' time, when computers have taken over most of human thinking, no other word will be more important. But PO does not yet exist in language. It may be impossible for such a word to exist. I believe otherwise. I believe that PO can take its place in language and thought, and that is why I am writing this book.

magic

PO is a magic word. It will do all you want it to do if you believe in it. As with all magic, the more you believe the better it works. The more you invest in it the more you get out of it. But there is no dogma you have to accept before you can use PO. It is a simple word, and all you have to believe in is its use.

mathematics

Unlike all other magic words, PO works best if in addition to believing in it you also understand what it is all about. PO is the first word ever to arise directly from the mathematics of the mind. PO is based on science, not on philosophical speculation. The way the mind works as a thinking machine makes the word PO essential. This may be why the PO concept has made sense to scientists and mathematicians who have come across it. But PO makes as much sense to artists.

problems

Population, pollution, poverty, political polarization, and the other problems that threaten humanity are going to get worse rather than better. In order to tackle these problems at the most fundamental level, we are going to have to improve our thinking and change our ideas before it is too late. There is no level of action more fundamental than our thinking habits. The purpose of PO is to provide something we have always lacked – a method for changing ideas. That is why PO or something like it is so necessary to help solve the problems of today and tomorrow.

first step

PO is but one word. But one word can be very powerful if it enables us to do things that are not easy without it. PO is a first step in a new direction. Once you have taken the PO step other things will follow, for it is the first step into a new world that is always the most difficult.

no persuasion

I am not going to try to persuade anyone to use PO. It is not difficult to prove the necessity for PO, but, as we shall see, proof is not persuasion. I regard PO as an opportunity, and I see no reason for forcing an opportunity on someone. I shall explain what PO is about and give some idea of what can be done with it. What happens next is up to you. You can ignore PO and walk by, having lost nothing and having gained nothing. You can seek to prove that PO does not exist or you can try out PO to see what you yourself can do with it.

tool

PO is a thinking tool. If you come across a new tool that has proved useful to other people, you may want to see if you can learn to use it yourself. But there is no obligation to do so.

PO People and NOPO People

PO *people and* NOPO *people*

The world is divided into two sorts of people: the PO people and the NOPO people. Only they do not know it yet. You yourself will not know whether you are a PO person or a NOPO person until you have finished reading this book. At the end you will have a very clear idea, because you will either understand PO or hate it. You will also be able to look around at your friends, your family, your boss, the people you work with, your politicians, and any other people in your life and decide whether they are PO people or NOPO people.

categories

When you have finished reading the book you will see at once into which of the following categories you fit as regards your reaction to PO:

1. Find it so contrary to your nature that you could simply never begin to understand it.
2. Understand it and hate it.
3. Feel very threatened by it and therefore hostile.
4. Understand and agree with it but find it difficult to use.
5. Find it easy to use both as an attitude of mind and also as a specific tool in thinking.
6. Find that it crystallizes and focuses in a sharp manner ideas you have always had.

In short, you will find whether you are a PO person or a NOPO person. The peculiarity of the PO/NOPO division is that NOPO people can change and become PO people if they make the effort. But PO people can never lose their PO quality to become NOPO people. That is because PO has to do with creativity.

PO groups

Over the last two years I have had the reaction to the PO concept from forty thousand people. It has been fascinating to see how the reaction to PO differs from group to group. The division has been as follows:

Those who see the need for PO: poets, painters, sculptors, architects, designers, mathematicians, computer scientists, physicists, teachers (some), children, students, young people in general, journalists, photographers, bankers, business executives.

Those who don't: politicians, philosophers, lawyers, academics, teachers (some), and literary critics.

The division seems to be between those who are actually involved in doing something and producing new ideas and those who are too busy defending already established ideas to see the need for new ones. It is a division between those who are looking to the future and those who are looking to the past. That may be why young people have shown so much interest.

strange bedfellows

There are few things which unite hippies and big-business corporations, painters and mathematicians. The need for new ideas does just this. The traditional divisions between art and science, young and old, pleasure and business, are cut right across by the reaction to the PO concept. The new division has on one side all those interested in creativity and new ideas and on the other side those who feel threatened by them.

angry

The PO concept upsets a lot of people, who get very angry about it. There are certain minds which prefer rigidity to flexibility, security to exploration, and they feel that their security is threatened by PO. They will also resent a tool which they themselves may not be very good at using. This book is not designed to make such people angry, but it will no doubt have exactly that effect.

not difficult but different

PO is not at all difficult, but it is different. No matter how fluent you may become at speaking Italian you will not suddenly find yourself speaking Yugoslav. In the same way, you may be very clever in the old style of thinking and yet fail completely to understand PO. Someone else who is not officially so clever may be able to understand PO at once. Understanding something difficult is a matter of effort. But understanding something different requires not effort but a willingness to accept new ideas.

Change and the Future

stop the future

We have been given a taste of the future and we do not like it, because we cannot see how we are going to cope with it. Books like Alvin Toffler's *Future Shock* have spelled out the future in all its difficulty. But complaining about the future will not stop it. The more change there is, the more chaos will there be, since chaos is caused by differing rates of change in different parts of the system. For instance, medicine lets more babies live and keeps people alive longer. There is then chaos until improved food supplies and birth control catch up. Cheaper food means mechanization on the farms, which means a population drift to the towns and problems until urban organization catches up. You cannot stop the future by reversing medicine and letting more people die or by making agriculture inefficient to keep people on the land.

too many new ideas

There are those who claim that we need fewer new ideas rather than more, since we seem unable to cope with the ones we have. They point to the atomic bomb, to industrial pollution, to supersonic airliners, to show the harm of new ideas. But the atomic bomb is the result of a very old idea: make your weapons as powerful as possible. Supersonic airliners are the result of a very old idea: travel as fast as possible. Industrial pollution is the result of a very old idea: throw things away and forget about them. It is not the new ideas that are harmful but the old ideas that so badly need changing.

technological thinking

You have only to look at the fantastic success of the moon shots and the advances in medicine and food production to see that our scientific and technological thinking is highly effective. But this is a very special sort of thinking involving defined objectives achieved by experiment, mathematics, and measurement. But human affairs cannot be treated in the same way, because human values are not subject to mathematics and are also unstable. In technological thinking you move steadily ahead from idea to idea, but in thinking about human affairs you may have to step backwards and escape from ideas which were valid enough in their time but are now obstacles to progress.

gap

As suggested earlier, chaos results when different parts of the system change at different rates. Our technology has changed, but our basic thinking tools, outside mathematics, have not changed for thousands of years. Our old-fashioned thinking system is inadequate to cope with present-day demands or to create a future. There is a gap between the system we have and the one we need.

the future

To look at the future only in terms of what is going to happen to population, pollution, productivity, cities, and morals is not enough. To dissolve what we have into chaos is not a way of building something new. To complain about the dissolution is also not a way of building something new. We need to look at something that is basic to all our problems, and that is our thinking system.

cures, not complaints

Instead of complaining about the future it is better to try and do something about it. Books like Charles Reich's *The Greening of America* are hopes that people will naturally come to change their priorities. This is wishful thinking and at best a passive hope. I think we need more specific tools for dealing with the future than passive hopes. For instance, in our thinking system we have never developed any tool for changing ideas except conflict.

Old Think

end of an intellectual era

We came to the end of an intellectual era some years ago. This was the end of the era that had started so long ago with the ancient Greek philosophers. The end of the era was not recognized in any formal way, because the traditional intellectuals whose business it is to note such changes are themselves too much part of the old era to notice them. Also you cannot notice the passing of one era except by heralding the beginning of a new one – and that we have been unable to do. Some time ago I was asked by the *New York Times* to review a book on modern

American philosophy. I was very shocked to find that it consisted only of the traditional word-dances and concept-knitting. That is to say, 'nun's' knitting carried out solely for the exquisite pleasure of the knitter and the envy of other knitters but of no practical use.

academic irrelevance

The universities used to be the centres of thinking, but they are now dropping out of the scene. To many people they have become irrelevant centres of mental masturbation. The old-style intellectual habits have no relevance to the modern world. For instance, 'scholarship' has become little more than the triumph of form over content. You take some tiny part of the field of knowledge and examine it with immense detail and concentration. In the end it is your workmanship which is praised and not the importance of the subject. This was commendable when society was stable and mental virtuosity of this sort had as much validity as exquisite chamber music. At that time the concept of usefulness was ugly and inferior. Better to tackle a useless subject which you could examine in depth than try and cope with a useful subject which was so large as to make impossible an impressive display of scholarship detail. Academic irrelevance is often a reality. It is no fault of the people involved but a direct result of the thinking system we have outgrown. The academic idiom was established to look backwards and preserve the past, not to look forwards and create the future.

no progress

If we compare the progress we have made in the technological sphere with the lack of progress we have made in the human sphere, then it seems likely that there is an inadequacy in our thinking system. We still have the same wars, hatreds, polarizations, persecutions, only now they can be carried out by modern weapons.

Old Think and New People

self-fulfilling system

Some academics do not see the irrelevance of the old-style thinking system, because they live in a self-fulfilling environment where they create the values they wish to esteem. But young people who have more contact with the outside world as regards their present and future lives can see the irrelevance more clearly. But not always. I have seen the tragedy of many fresh young minds crippled by the arrogance and rigidity of the old system.

rigid system

Old-style thinking insists on fixed concepts, certainties and absolutes. These are processed by means of traditional logic, and the answers are treated with the arrogance and dogmatism which always accompany academic logic. There is nothing wrong with the logic as such, but, as in scholarship, the emphasis is on the perfection of the processing and not on the basic concepts used. Another important danger is the smugness that follows perfect logic and excludes the search for new ideas and better approaches. Yet another danger is that you tackle only that part of the situation that can be tackled with precision and ignore the rest as if it did not exist.

old-style thinking and the real world

Equipped with this old-style thinking, young people try to understand the real world. But they find that their equipment is inadequate. For one thing, the old system does not teach them how to deal with uncertainties, because everything has been cut and dried and proved in absolute terms. They also find that they have been equipped to defend ideas but have not been given any tools for changing ideas. Finally, they find that logic is fine after you have chosen your basic concepts, but it is with these that all the difficulty arises. Culture has trapped them with a huge number of fixed concepts from which they are not equipped to escape in order to see things in a different way.

crisis of confidence

If you have been brought up with rigid ideas, then with the first crack these fall apart and leave nothing. Rigidity and dogmatism give permanence up to a point, but beyond that point they give brittleness.

flight and fight

When they find that the old-style thinking system is not adequate to deal with the modern world, the young react in different ways. There are those who seek to escape with drugs which do not help them to understand the world but make it seem less important that they should try. Another reaction is to find sense in the world by supposing that it is organized by some outside system such as astrology or hidden forces. Then there are those who express their frustration in mindless attack because only in attack can they find any direction, purpose, and sense.

PO and People

Feeling

disillusioned

Young people have come to prefer feeling to thinking. They have become disillusioned with academic thinking because of its arid irrelevance, because it can be used to defend whatever point of view you like (to stay in Vietnam or get out, to support West Pakistan or Bangla Desh, to be for or against apartheid), and especially because they find that life does not fit into neat logical equations. In place of thinking they have put 'feeling'. They believe that if they feel strongly enough about anything (Vietnam, ghettos, environment) all will be well. Feeling is seen as being more valid than the fancy word games of thinking.

feeling and priorities

The emphasis on feeling rather than thinking is a necessary one because academic thinking has indeed tended to become an artificial game in itself without relevance to real life. Body counts in the war were just numbers on paper to be juggled with and not real people. Pollution was a necessary cost of industrialization and not real rivers with real dead fish. Since man is the centre of man's world it must be his collective feelings that matter most in the end. It must be feeling that decides priorities: whether to shoot for the moon or to clear up slums. Feeling sets priorities, gives direction, and provides pressures.

not enough

Unfortunately, feeling by itself is not enough to get things done. You need organization to channel the energy of feeling, and ideas to give it form. Feeling strongly enough about cities does not actually reorganize them. Nor is a nostalgic escape back to the pure world of nature much good, because the pure world of nature is not nearly as idyllic as many people seem to think: the strong prey on the weak, and everyone looks after himself or his own small herd.

feelings and ideas

There was a bad famine in a rice-eating country. The relief organizations managed to fly in a large quantity of maize. The starving people preferred to go on starving rather than eat the maize, for they had the 'idea' that maize was food for animals. Ideas are much more powerful than feelings because they direct feelings. It is an idea that sends people to be burned alive at the stake. It is an idea that makes people go willingly to the stake in martyrdom. Ideas in Northern Ireland cause people to hate each other to the point of killing. Ideas on birth control may decide the fate of man. Feelings are fine if they are going in the 'right' direction, but if they are sent off in the wrong direction by ideas it is the ideas that have to be changed first. And changing ideas requires both thinking and feeling. Thinking is no use without feeling, but feeling is no substitute for thinking. Instead of abandoning thinking we need to put feeling back into it. The more intelligent young people realize this full well.

Old Think and New Think

process and perception

The old-style thinking system was mainly concerned with processing ideas. You started off with accepted concepts and then put them together in the authorized way to reach a conclusion.

It was always assumed that the starting concepts were valid since they were the established way of looking at the situation. Thus, crime must be looked at in terms of criminals and guilt. Poverty must be looked at in terms of personal human failure. In contrast, the new-style thinking system is more concerned with the starting concepts themselves than with the processing of them. The new-style thinking system is more concerned with the way things are looked at – with perception. And this is where feeling comes in. Feeling plays little part in logical processing, but it plays a major part in perception. PO is the tool of this new-style thinking just as YES and NO are the tools of the old-style thinking.

the bridge and the river

A bridge is a solid immovable structure that serves a useful purpose. It is the sort of rigid structure produced by old-style thinking. YES and NO are the tools which build such definite structures by fitting one block on top of another. The river which flows beneath the bridge also has a definite shape, but it is not a rigid shape like the bridge. Yet the river can also be useful – especially in generating power. If too much load is placed on the bridge it cracks and falls apart and is destroyed. But an obstructed river adapts and reforms itself into a different shape. You cannot build up a river by fitting pieces together or take it apart in the same way, because it is the whole that has shape. But you can change that shape. The river is like the new-style thinking, and PO is the tool for changing its shape. So the opposite of rigidity and shape is not chaos or shapelessness but a new sort of shape.

optimism

If the human race was really as bright as it thinks it is there would be little hope for the future. But I believe we are only just beginning a new era in which our thinking system is going to change more than it has changed in the last two thousand years. PO is a step in this direction.

The Nature of PO

PO *as thinking tool*

It is incredible that outside mathematics we have not invented any new thinking tools since the days of Aristotle. PO is a deliberate invention of a thinking tool.

PO *as skill*

The use of PO is a skill which can be learned and practised just as you learn to drive, cook, surf or play golf. In fact, PO makes it possible to acquire as a skill thinking habits which otherwise depend on chance and temperament.

PO *as reverse gear*

PO is like the reverse gear in a car. Without a reverse gear you get blocked in the first blind alley you come to. And culturally this is exactly what has happened in so many areas. The reverse gear is not a substitute for the forward gears but necessary in addition. So PO is necessary in addition to the other thinking skills such as mathematics. Only a fool would try to drive on the reverse gears all the time, but only a fool would design a car without one. It is not how much you use the reverse gear that matters but the ability to use it when necessary. A car without a reverse gear is useless except for following well-known circular tracks.

PO *as change tool*

PO is directly concerned with new ideas, new approaches, and the escape from concept prisons. Concept prisons are traditional fixed ideas which prevent us from looking at something in a new way. For instance, the concept of 'school' is a concept prison because it makes it difficult to think of other ways in which education can happen. Perhaps education should be built into the environment much more consciously. The concept of 'schoolchildren' also makes us think of education as happening to children. This shuts out such ideas as split education. There could be education up to the age of fifteen and then another short period at twenty-five and again at forty-five and sixty. These short periods would be six months or a year. The idea would be to equip people directly for the years ahead of them. Thus, the needs of a fifteen-year-old are different from the needs and interests of a sixty-year-old. It would also give people more opportunity to change their lives and jobs instead of having them fixed at an early age when there is nothing on which to base the choice.

PO *and creativity*

PO is a thinking tool that is as basic to creative thinking as NO is to logical thinking.

PO *and creative reserves*

PO can unlock latent creative reserve. Most people are unable to use their creative reserves, because there is no key with which to unlock the door that has been locked by traditional educational rigidity.

PO *as laxative*

PO can be used as a laxative for those who have constipated minds that they wish to free.

PO *and humour*

PO is very directly related to humour, as will be shown later. The ability to understand and use PO is closely related to a sense of humour. With humour you go beyond the obvious to seek new ways of looking at things, in exactly the same way as you do with PO.

PO *and children*

The three intellectual ages of man could be described as follows.

    0 – 5   years: the age of WHY?
    5 – 10   years: the age of WHY NOT?
    10 – 75 + years: the age of BECAUSE

Before five, children are still collecting information by asking 'Why?' There is as yet too little information with which to be creative. Between five and ten is the only creative period in the lives of most people. This is the age in which children try out new ideas and new ways of looking at the world. Nor is it the creativity of ignorance, because children in this age group will seek to improve even such familiar objects as a house or a bicycle. I have a collection of thousands of young children's drawings which show this effect most clearly. But after the age of ten education insists that children adopt the established way of looking at things and do things only as they 'should be done'. Creativity no longer counts, imitation and acceptance are what matter. PO acts to keep the age of WHY NOT going alongside the age of BECAUSE which society does need in order to have competence. In adults PO can serve to resurrect the child's creative way of looking at things.

PO *and difference*

Education usually works on the matching system. That is to say if the pupil's output matches what is expected it is marked right: if it does not match it is marked wrong. There is no way of distinguishing what is wrong in itself from what is merely different. This fault is not special to education but is inevitable in any system that works on a matching basis – including computers.

PO *is reasonable*

PO is perfectly reasonable – but completely illogical. We have been trained to believe that the absence of logic is chaos, confusion, and even madness, but it is not. PO is certainly illogical, but nevertheless it is very reasonable, as we shall see later. We have been brainwashed over the ages to believe that logic is the only way of handling ideas in order to reach a useful result.

PO *is a de-patterning device*

PO acts to break down established patterns, PO acts to introduce discontinuity. One of the major functions of PO is as an anti-arrogance and anti-dogmatism device.

PO *and you*

Different people will react to PO in very different ways. Some people will find that PO opens up a whole new world of thinking. Some will find it is just the sort of device they have been looking for to liberate them from the rigidity and arrogance of the YES/NO system. Some will use it as a symbol or banner to indicate their feelings and crystallize their attitudes. Some will use it simply as a direct tool for creative problem-solving. Some may regard it as a philosophy or even a religion. Provided you are a PO person, the way you treat PO depends more on you than on PO itself. It depends on whether you want to open yourself to new ideas and whether you can escape from the cramping rigidity of your education in the YES/NO system. PO is a neutral tool. How you use it tells as much about you as about the tool.

PO Basis

tripod basis

There are three separate reasons for introducing the new word
PO. Each one of these reasons would be sufficient by itself. Together they form a firm tripod.

1. To correct the deficiencies, limitations, and dangers of the
   old-style thinking system with its YES/NO basis.
2. To enable us to make more effective use of the patterning
   behaviour of the brain.
3. To provide the creative tool which we have always lacked.

PO Thinking

The Basis of Old Think

three disasters

It could be said that the three greatest intellectual disasters to befall the mind of Western man were:

1. The ancient Greeks
2. The Renaissance
3. The Crucifixion

the ancient Greek philosophers

The ancient Greeks lived in a static society. They directed their thinking to creating concepts and then refining them to such a point of perfection that they would never need changing. Instead of the uncertainty of experiment and observation, they preferred the certainty of logic to create truths. Ideas were treated much as a child might treat coloured blocks on a table. They were played with and moved around and fitted together. The game was logic, and the basic tools of this game were YES and NO, which indicated whether the arrangements were permissible or not. New concepts were produced either by taking apart existing concepts in the process called analysis or by fitting them together to give bigger concepts. The result was a sharp, precise, and self-contained thinking system that examined the relationship between static and fixed concepts. This was a system that was not capable of evolution and not designed to cope with change.

the Renaissance

The Renaissance moved the mind of man out of the Dark Ages during which thinking consisted only in repeating the ideas that were held the day before and action was directed by ritual, mystery, and immediate feeling. In place of this repetition idiom the Renaissance revived the Greek search-and-establish idiom. This meant the search for eternal truths, for absolute ideals, and for the fixed order that was assumed to underly everything. All the time ideas were moving forward towards these absolutes. There was no provision in the thinking system for stepping back from an idea that had once been right in order to develop a new way of looking at things. Even advances such as those of Kepler and Galileo arose from a need to arrange the heavenly spheres in a more perfect order. In art, perspective was developed with its fixed lines and rigid rules in order to make pictures as close to perfect reality as possible. Art would still be imprisoned today by perspective had the camera not come along and taken over the picture function of art, so freeing it to go beyond the obvious and explore ideas. To explore ideas art went back to pre-Renaissance primitivism to find energy and new directions. In the same way as the camera freed art, so today the computer frees thinking from its Renaissance prison by taking over the mechanical YES/NO function and freeing the mind of man for creativity. Freed in this way we can start to go beyond the obvious in our way of looking at things, just as did the artists when they were freed from their Renaissance prison. Instead of the static system of fixed order dictated by the Renaissance we can start moving towards more dynamic sorts of order. That is exactly what PO is about.

the Crucifixion

The Crucifixion was a disaster because it established attitudes which were quite contrary to Christianity itself and have cramped Christianity ever since. Christianity opened up man's attitudes to his fellow men in terms of love and tolerance. The Crucifixion, however, emphasized the sharp polarization of 'good' and 'evil' that put all the intolerance into the practical administration of Christianity. The Crucifixion made fear, sin, and guilt the motive force. It also bred the arrogance, righteousness, and dogmatism that are the other side of the polarization. The world might have been a better place if somehow the Crucifixion had simply been dropped out of Christian teaching, because once it was there it was so powerful that it had to become the central point. It would then have been necessary to demonstrate divine love by living example rather than by reference to an historic death. It is interesting that religions like Islam and Buddhism which have no equivalent to the Crucifixion have always been more tolerant. The Crucifixion allowed thinkers to emphasize the sharp YES/NO exclusivity and to build a dangerous arrogance and certainty on this. Christianity itself was much more PO than YES/NO.

The YES/NO System

effective

The YES/NO system is the basis of the old-style thinking system. There is no doubt that it is an effective system. You have only to look around at the technical progress we have made in order to see its effectiveness. But in terms of human behaviour and human happiness we might have been very much better off if we had developed a different thinking system. Or at least we might have been better off if we had combined the rigid selective effectiveness of the YES/NO system with a creative factor like PO which facilitates change and removes the main dangers of rigidity. In a pure YES/NO system there are serious dangers and limitations.

the basic tool NO

NO is the basic tool of logical thinking. It works in a simple and direct manner. We look at an idea and if it does not fit our experience we use NO to throw out that idea. NO indicates a mismatch between an idea and our experience. If we have set up a number system so that $2 + 2 = 4$ we cannot accept the idea that $2 + 2 = 5$, because that does not fit our experience, so we use NO to throw the idea out. We deal in the same way with the idea that eggs are square, that dogs have five legs, and that Napoleon won at Waterloo.

NO is a preservative

NO preserves the ideas that have been established by experience. In the same way NO preserves a way of looking at things that has been established and protects it from change. If you happened to be in Chicago at the Democratic convention in 1968 and saw 'anarchists attacking the police' you would reject anything which conflicted with that idea. But if instead you saw 'young idealists brutally attacked by the police' you would also reject anything which did not fit with that idea. The YES/NO system works only to preserve the established way of looking at things. For instance, if someone were to suggest that criminals ought to be paid a pension, you would reject the idea because it does not fit the established idea of guilt and punishment. The first limitation of the YES/NO system is that it preserves ideas and is of no help in changing them – it has no creative ability whatsoever.

sharp polarization

I was a witness at the famous Oz trial at the Old Bailey, and at one point in this trial the judge stated there were only three ways of answering a question : 'Yes,' 'No,' or 'I don't know.' The YES/NO system leads to sharp and artificial polarizations that are dangerous because they create simple rigid judgements for complex situations. The YES/NO system is an amplifier of small differences because it works only with extremes. You are asked to decide whether something can be rejected or accepted. At once rejection becomes complete rejection, and acceptance becomes complete acceptance. You have no choice but to move immediately to either extreme. Something is black or it is white, someone is a friend or an enemy. The major defect of our type of democracy is that the system is based directly on the YES/NO polarization.

Because voting is on the YES/NO basis people in opposing parties have to take opposite attitudes whether they personally agree with them or not, in order to polarize the voters' choice. The effect is to polarize people even beyond their own natural tendencies.

contradiction

In the YES/NO system two contradictory statements cannot both be right at the same time. A thing cannot be totally black and totally white, a figure cannot be a perfect square and a perfect circle at the same time. It is a very fundamental principle of the system that contradictions are not allowed. This is so basic that we often feel that proving the error of an opposite point of view proves the correctness of our own point of view. This intolerance of contradiction makes the YES/NO system unsuitable for dealing with human values, for here the same thing may have opposite values to different people or even to the same person in different moods. In the PO system contradictions are allowed.

fixed ideas and boxes

The rigidity of the YES/NO system tends to fix ideas. It produces 'box' definitions. Something is either inside the box or outside it. An animal is either a dog or it is not. A nation is an aggressor or it is not. Society has freedom or it does not. Language needs such rigid definitions, otherwise communication would be impossible. But thinking does not need them, for rigid box definitions make the slow evolution of ideas impossible since an idea cannot drift in or out of a definition but must at all times be inside or outside. For instance, a situation in which someone freely chooses constraints as an expression of his freedom is difficult to consider.

certainty

In the YES/NO system we proceed from one certainty to the next one so that when we reach a conclusion that also is certain. This means that we cannot proceed unless we have certainty. So when

31

we do not have certainty we simply counterfeit it and soon forget that we have done so. Since the YES/NO system is fuelled by certainty we manufacture it for ourselves whenever we need it.

arrogance

If you have put together ideas in such a way that you yourself cannot insert a NO, then you have to believe that you are absolutely right. In fact, you may feel so right that you regard it as your duty to impose your idea on someone else even if it means physically forcing him to accept your idea. It cannot occur to you that your right idea is 'right' only in terms of the concept package with which you started out. The YES/NO system simply has no provision for such considerations. Thus, if your concept package includes carnal desire, sin, lust, temptation, sex, then you are logically right to insist that Polynesian women must wear brassières and not let their breasts hang free. The same logic applies whether you are the first missionary to visit Hawaii or the local authorities giving a permit to a troupe of African dancers.

another idea

If your idea is right and therefore has the arrogance of logic but someone else has a different idea, then clearly his idea must be wrong. Otherwise the YES/NO system loses its main advantage, its selective value. With the YES/NO system it is very difficult to accept two different ideas as both being right.

smugness

Since an idea that is right is absolutely right, there can be no point in going further to look for a better idea. Thus the smugness of logic cuts off creative exploration by making it unnecessary. If you know that cholera must be caused by the evil smell from sewers, why should you look further for other causes? With almost every scientific advance the person with the new idea had a very hard time convincing those who held logically adequate ideas that they should look at new ones. One man had to drink a glassful of active cholera germs to prove his point, and another had to infect himself with syphilis.

oil and vinegar

My favourite problem for showing the arrogance of logic involves a glass of oil placed next to a glass of vinegar. You take a spoonful of oil and stir it into the vinegar glass. Next you take a spoonful of the mixture and put it back into the oil glass. The question is whether you now have more oil in the vinegar glass or more vinegar in the oil glass. Logic is quick to point out that an exchange of pure oil for a mixture must leave more oil in the vinegar glass. But logic is quite wrong. Nevertheless many highly intelligent people will support with extraordinary arrogance this conclusion which has been reached by logic.

the positive YES

In mathematics, computers, and logic the important word is NO. If something does not fit or breaks the rules it is rejected. Everything which is not rejected is automatically accepted without any special acceptance label. Such systems could really do without YES, because what is not labelled NO is always YES. But in real life YES is much more than the simple absence of NO. YES has a very strong emotional basis. YES is the basic tool of the belief system. With beliefs it is not just a matter of not saying NO but of saying YES, YES, YES a thousand times. This very real positive value of YES is usually forgotten in considering the YES/NO system, but it adds very much to the rigidity and arrogance of the system and makes it especially difficult to change ideas. If the emotional YES did not exist, then the simplest NO would be enough to reject a current idea and bring about a change to a better one. But in practice you have to build up a very powerful and almost emotional NO in order to challenge an emotion-based YES. Mere evidence is not enough. That is why fluoridation of water and birth control are not universal.

based on action not thinking

The YES/NO system is based directly on two things. The first thing is the way our eyes see the world. We see it divided up into separate objects. These objects are either there or not there. The objects are either similar or not similar. From all this we get the principle of 'identity' and 'non-identity' which underlies all logic. The second basis of the YES/NO system is the need for action. Since it is useless to act in a half-hearted manner, the YES/NO system polarizes judgement to extremes. You cannot eat and not eat a piece of bread. You must eat it in a definite manner, and if you are not definite enough about getting the bread in the first place you may not even survive. You cannot jump and not jump out of the way of a car, or you may not survive. Survival depends on being definite and certain, and the YES/NO system provides this certainty.

thinking is different

But the needs of action are not the same as the needs of thinking. In thinking it may, for instance, be necessary to go through an idea that is wrong in order to reach a new idea that is right. But you cannot do this in action. You can think about a man walking through fire and come up with an idea for a fire-resistant suit. But if you actually had to walk through the fire first you would be too dead to design any such suit. The YES/NO system is designed more for action than for thinking. That is why the system has served us well so far, but today we need to do rather more thinking before action than we have had to in the past, simply because the problems are greater.

PO is designed for the creative thinking that comes before action.

thinking and language

The YES/NO system is also well suited to language because communication requires precision and certainty. This is why ordinary language is not really suitable for thinking. In thinking it may sometimes be necessary to use vague or 'blurry' ideas as stepping-stones or links. The function and importance of such 'blurry' ideas are described in my book *Practical Thinking* (Cape, 1971).

No Tools for Change

people outlive ideas

In the past, ideas have always lived longer than people. Once they were established, ideas would be changed only slowly and over several generations. But today technology and science have so speeded up the rate of change in the world that for the first time ever people actually live longer than ideas. This means that for the first time people need to change their ideas within their life-time in order to keep up with the world. Unfortunately we have never developed any tools at all for changing ideas in this way.

establish, not change

Our whole thinking system has been designed to establish and prove the truth of ideas. We have never developed tools for changing ideas, because it has always seemed inconceivable that the ideas we hold at the moment should ever need changing. The ideas we hold at the moment must be right, otherwise we should not hold them. And right ideas cannot need changing. The whole basis of the Greek/Renaissance system is that you progress from the right ideas you hold to a refinement of these as you get closer and closer to a perfect perception of underlying reality. You can move forward from a right idea but never backward to find a better idea. The whole YES/NO system is designed to preserve and defend ideas and to reject any attempt to change them.

change through rejection

With the YES/NO system change can come about only if the current idea is rejected. An idea must definitely be shown to be

35

wrong before there can be any question of changing it or even considering the need to change it.

confrontation and clash

Since change can be achieved only by rejecting the current idea, any new idea must take the form of an attack on the old idea. The defenders of the old idea hasten to resist and to reject the threatening new idea because it does not fit into the old way of looking at things. So the old idea becomes strengthened in defence and the new idea becomes more forceful in attack. In the end there is a head-on clash between the new idea and the old idea. This process was shown beautifully when naval designers started to put forward the 'ridiculous' idea of ships driven by screws instead of paddle-wheels. In the end the clash between the new idea and the old idea was settled by an actual tug of war. In this a screw-driven ship towed a much more powerful paddle steamer backwards through the water. Rarely is the clash so neat or the outcome so decisive. Usually the ideas meet head on in bloody revolution, and for practical purposes one or the other idea triumphs and the remaining idea is subdued – but neither one is changed. This is the 'swap' system that has been our chief method for political, cultural, or religious changes. In this swap system two opposing ideas grow ever more rigid and fierce until they meet in a head-on clash.

too dangerous

The swap system does work, but usually in a bloody manner. Today society is too complex and weapons too powerful for the old-fashioned swap system to be anything but highly dangerous to everyone on both sides. Even on an internal basis the system can no longer work, because those in power have too great a technological advantage over those seeking power. This means the latter can only be destructive without any real hope of achieving a swap.

thesis and antithesis

Sometimes the clash system is used deliberately as a mental tool in an effort to generate new ideas. One idea is set up as the thesis and then the opposite idea is set up as the antithesis. This is the dialectical system, and from the clash between thesis and antithesis is supposed to emerge a new idea as a synthesis. Although much talked about, it is a most ineffective method, for the basic concepts involved remain unchanged on both sides. At best one achieves a patchwork effect and perhaps some alteration in values but nothing really creative. That is why Communism (based on the dialectical system) is old-fashioned, bureaucratic, and authoritarian, when it set out to be the opposite to all these things. The dialectical system is not creative, because, like the YES/NO system itself, it is a second-stage thinking process that accepts the basic concepts and simply reshuffles them. ('Power' goes to the workers instead of to the capitalists, but the concept of 'power' remains.)

scientific method

It is only in science that the clash system of change works tolerably well. In science you reinforce the new idea with so much evidence that it triumphs over the old one. Even so the defence of the old idea is fierce, and most important scientific ideas have been accepted only long after they were first suggested. The clash method in science works only because the new evidence can be assessed by objective and repeatable measurement.

outside science

Outside science the clash method does not work, because new evidence cannot be measured objectively but has to be looked at and assessed through the old ideas. Looking through these old ideas you can see only material which agrees with those ideas or disagrees. The material which disagrees is by definition wrong. Without objective measurement you have no choice except to

37

judge subjectively; and you can judge subjectively only by using the only available framework for judgement – current ideas. Thus even an idea which is so right that it will eventually create a new framework must at first be rejected when looked at through the existing framework.

even more difficult

It is bad enough when an idea resists change because it cannot be faulted when looked at in the old way, but it is worse than that. Often it is impossible to change an idea that *can* be faulted. This is because ideas are affirmed not simply on logical grounds but also on emotional grounds. This means that the YES which affirms them is not simply the absence of NO but satisfies some emotional need. A person who is determined to believe in flying saucers travels to Norway to examine the wreck of a saucer that is said to have crashed there. If he finds nothing, then clearly the wreckage has been removed by the government in order to pretend it never happened. If he finds the wreckage of an ordinary plane, then clearly the government has substituted the plane deliberately to mislead the investigators. So lack of actual evidence for the flying saucer is actually evidence of the conspiracy to hush it up and hence evidence for the saucers, since you do not hush up something which is not true. There is really no way of changing this sort of idea (other than PO), and the idea becomes an impregnable myth which resists all evidence to destroy it.

too slow

Quite apart from its dangers and inefficiency, the clash system of change is very, very slow. It is slow because you have to wait until ideas are obviously wrong and falling apart before you even try to look for new ideas. It is slow because you do not actually set out to look for new ideas but wait for them to happen. It is slow because the old idea sets about defending itself and rejecting the new idea for as long as possible.

no change tool

The truth is that we have simply never tried to develop any thinking tool for changing ideas. On the contrary, our thinking is based on the YES/NO system which is an anti-change system. That is why the introduction of PO as a deliberate change tool is so very necessary in our culture.

instead of clash

The YES/NO system has led to the development of 'clash' as our major method of change because truth and untruth are pitted against each other with the usual certainty on both sides. There are, however, many other methods of change. In the by-pass method an alternative channel is created alongside the existing channel. If it proves useful it widens with use and eventually comes to divert flow from the original channel. In the increment method a small change gradually alters the whole system. An amazing example of this occurred with the development of consumerism in the United States from Ralph Nader's first book. In the insight method a new way of looking at things which makes sense at once simply evaporates the established position. There are many further methods.

Education

based on the old thinking system

Education is very firmly based on the old thinking system. In most academic circles it is considered to be the highest form of intellectual achievement to think like the ancient Greeks. While we have made progress in every other field, it is considered to be a matter of great pride that over more than two thousand years we have made no progress at all in developing new thinking tools.

pass on ideas

Education has always considered its duty to be the passing on intact of established ideas. Education has never regarded it as its duty to question these ideas, alter them, or even provide tools for changing them.

dogmatism

Education has usually encouraged dogmatism for the very practical reason that dogmatism seemed the most effective way of transferring ideas from the teacher to the taught. If an idea was to be treated as dogma, then both teacher and student were relieved of the necessity to do any thinking about it.

arrogance of logic

Since education is a closed and highly artificial world, it is never possible to check the validity of an idea to see how it relates to the real world. Instead the only criterion of validity is the logic by which the idea has been derived and with which it is defended. So logic is equated with truth, and this gives logic an unjustified arrogance which outlasts education.

need to be right

From the earliest age there is the absolute insistence in education on the need to be right all the time. Encouragement and approval, which are emotionally necessary to young children, are used only as rewards for being right. Being wrong means being rejected by the teacher. Later on, when this emotional support from the teacher is less important, being right is still tied directly to the child's self-esteem. Status in the class is tied to being right. Being wrong is a matter for shame. In this way being right all the time acquires a huge importance in education, and there is this terror of being wrong. The ego is so tied to being right that later on in life you are reluctant to accept that you are ever wrong, because you are defending not the idea but your self-esteem. Since in the clash system the only way to change an idea is to admit that it is wrong, this terror of being wrong means that people have enormous difficulty in changing ideas. How many politicians can you think of who would admit they were wrong on some issue and change their ideas – except after everyone else had done so?

difference

It was suggested previously that in a matching system there is no way of distinguishing between something that is different and something that is wrong. One of the major problems of education is dealing with differences: different ways of doing the same thing; different ways of looking at the same thing; different starting points, values, concepts, and background. The YES/NO system assumes a universal frame of reference and proceeds within this to demonstrate ultimate truths.

self-fulfilling

The education system is self-fulfilling, since those teachers are given posts whose ideas are most in line with the ideas of those giving out the posts. Education sets the exams that fit what it teaches and then prides itself that it has taught the right things for the exams.

poor job

On the whole, education does a poor job at equipping people to think. There are occasions when it seems that the better educated a person the less he is able to think. Specialized knowledge, facts, and the ability to quote opinions are not at all the same as skill in thinking.

obsolescence and new products

In order to avoid obsolescence an industry has to devote considerable sums to research for the development of new products.

41

In the same way education ought to be devoting a considerable part of its budget to developing new products like the thinking tool PO. But as a self-fulfilling system education is hardly aware of an obsolescence which is so obvious to everyone else.

Brain Patterns

First- and Second-Stage Thinking

perception and processing

Perception comes before processing in thinking. A wife discovers a red mark on her husband's handkerchief and accuses him of infidelity; actually he had used the handkerchief to wipe a crayon mark off the calendar. The winner of a major show-jumping event is disqualified because what he claims to be a victory sign is perceived by the judges as an insulting gesture. A driver stops to refill his radiator because the engine is overheating; actually it is overheating because the fan belt is broken. In each case an incorrect perception has led to an incorrect answer even though the thinking involved after the perception is perfectly correct.

perception and first stage

Traditionally we have been concerned only with the thinking that comes after perception. This is the second-stage thinking or processing of the situation that has been presented by perception. We have not paid too much attention to perception because we have believed that there could be only one way to look at things. But if you escape from the obvious way there are other ways to look at things and these other ways can be useful. I was staying in a country cottage and badly needed to iron a shirt. But there was no iron in that cottage. I could have gone out and borrowed one or even bought one if I had decided in the perception stage that an iron was needed. Instead my perception was different. So I heated a frying pan on the stove and then inserted it in a large brown paper envelope and proceeded to iron the shirt. Clearly the obvious perception of a frying pan is as a frying pan, but a different perception of the frying pan led to a different outcome. Another time I was visiting my old Oxford college for a celebration reunion and had great difficulty in buttoning a heavily starched dress shirt. So I removed a paperclip from some documents I had with me and used it as a buttonhook. Another change in perception.

profits

If your perception tells you that the sale of refrigerators is only a way to make profits for a few wealthy shareholders, then you might proceed to think of the inequities of capitalism. But if your perception tells you that profits are only a way of distributing useful refrigerators to people who need them, then you will proceed to think about ways of encouraging investment. If your perception tells you that the refrigerator is a device for transferring money from the buyers to the workers who make them, then you might proceed to think about the efficiency of this transfer. The important point is that your thinking is determined by your initial perceptions.

poverty

If you consider that poverty is due to human failure and laziness, then your next-stage thinking will consider how to penalize the poor or disregard them. If your perception tells you that poverty is an integral part of the free-enterprise system, then clearly that system has a responsibility to the poor.

obvious way

We have never regarded perception as thinking for two reasons:

1. Because we have always accepted that the obvious way of looking at things was the best and did not need thinking about.

2. Because the YES/NO system can work only after something has been produced by perception for it to work upon.

But if we believe that the obvious way of looking at things is not the only way or even the best one, then instead of taking perception for granted we have to treat it as the first stage of thinking and develop tools like PO for using in this first stage.

clock with no hands

In my lectures I often ask members of the audience to design a clock which has no moving features on its face and can still function effectively. They find this very difficult and come up with suggestions like a moving spot of light or a change in colour or a change in temperature. Yet the simple answer is an acoustical clock that tells the time by sound like a chiming grandfather clock or the telephone clock or a tape recorder. The trouble is that, having decided in the first stage, or perception stage, to look at a visual clock, they proceed in the second stage to design a visual clock without moving features.

frozen lock

I once came back from a skiing trip abroad to find that a blizzard had swept the car park at the airport and that the door locks on all the cars were so frozen up that it was impossible to insert a key. Everyone was busy trying to warm the locks by breathing on them, using hot water, or heating the key itself before inserting it. It was obvious that the first-stage thinking had decided that 'heat' was needed to release the locks. The second-stage thinking was then concerned with trying to find a way of applying this heat, and it was difficult because a strong wind was still blowing. But changing the first-stage concept from 'heat' to 'unfreeze' made the problem at once soluble. All I had to do was remember that many anti-freeze mixtures used alcohol and then pour into the lock a small amount of the duty-free brandy I had bought on the airliner. The lock unfroze at once as the alcohol lowered the freezing point. A simple change in perception made all the difference.

ambulance and sheep

An ambulance driving along a narrow country lane in a hurry comes up behind a flock of sheep that fills the lane. The situation seems quite obvious. The ambulance has to force its way past the sheep. So the shepherd must find a way of driving the flock off the road and into a field or else string them out along the sides of the road. Or the ambulance must drive very slowly and hope the sheep get out of the way. These are all alternative solutions turned up in the second stage of thinking once the first stage has decided that the problem is to get the ambulance past the sheep. But if you change your perception and instead of trying to get the ambulance past the sheep you try instead to get the sheep past the ambulance, then a new and simpler solution presents itself. You stop the ambulance and then turn the flock round and drive it backwards past the stationary ambulance so that the sheep find their way round it without risk of injury. Once the sheep have squeezed past, the road ahead is clear and the ambulance starts up and drives off.

concept package

At the end of the first stage of thinking we have a way of looking at the situation. This way of looking at the situation can be called the concept package. The second stage of thinking then goes to work on this concept package in order to produce a useful answer. The concept package contains three sorts of choice:

1. A choice as to which part of the situation is going to be considered.
2. A choice as to which concepts are going to be used.
3. A choice as to the values and priorities attached to the concepts used.

which part

If you look at the general problem of education you might consider different parts: the cost; the future cost if the present system continues; the effectiveness as related to the aims of the educators; the effectiveness as related to the needs of society; the efficiency of teachers; the ability of students; teacher–student interaction; acceptability of the type of education to the government; acceptability to the parents; acceptability to the students; the uniformity; the variety; the average student; the exceptional student, whether more gifted or more backward, etc. You could go on and on. It is not a matter of analysing the situation into a fixed number of component parts, because there is no fixed number. A new way of looking at the situation simply creates a new part. For instance, if I choose to look at education in terms of how much it blocks the natural self-education process of a child in society, I do not think this part of the situation would figure on the list of many educators. Nor would the idea that education may be training children in social maladjustment by exposing them to a society that no longer bears any relation to real society in terms of rigidity and the hierarchical system.

doctor

If you are looking at health care you might start out by choosing the concepts of 'hospital' and 'doctor', because these are the obvious concepts to use. But once you have chosen the concept of 'doctor', then your second-stage thinking is going to be concerned with educating doctors, paying doctors, recruiting more doctors, and giving them good working conditions. But doctors are very expensive to train, take a long time to train, wish to earn a high salary to compensate them for the long years of training, and prefer to work in pleasant surroundings. The second-stage thinking is all about doctors. But if you had chosen the concept 'medical worker', then you might have quickly got onto the idea of the medical auxiliaries who are used so very effectively in Russia. Doctors are expected to know about everything, and so their training has to be complete and expensive. A medical auxiliary has a much shorter training, because he is simply trained to deal effectively with a relatively few conditions which actually make up ninety per cent of medical care. You do not

47

need a doctor capable of diagnosing an acoustic neuroma (a rare form of brain tumour) to deal with a duodenal ulcer.

which values

If you take the Shakespearean story of Othello, who strangled his wife, Desdemona, because his friend had convinced him of her infidelity, you can see the huge difference made by values. You can work out the situation using the mathematics of conflict situations known as 'game theory', in order to see what Othello should have done. You are quite likely to come up with the mathematically correct answer that Othello ought to have strangled his wife and she on her part might as well have deceived him since she was going to be strangled anyway. This solution is, of course, determined entirely by the values you choose at the beginning: value of loss of face; value of smouldering suspicion and uncertainty; value of life to Desdemona; value of infidelity to Desdemona; value of Othello's belief in his friend; and so on. In most human situations it is precisely these values which are assigned in the first stage of thinking, or, more often, taken for granted, that really determine the solution – not the excellence of logical or mathematical processing in the second stage.

the YES/NO system and the second stage

Our main thinking system, the YES/NO system, is directed exclusively to the second stage of thinking. Once we have decided on the concept package, the YES/NO system helps us to sort it out and process it. This second-stage processing is carried out by logic (using the YES/NO system), by mathematics, or increasingly by computers. You feed your concept package into the computer and out comes the answer.

automatic first stage

There is usually no conscious thinking about the first stage, for it is taken as obvious. This is the way of looking at the situation that has been set up by experience, by culture, by society. It does not seem to be something you think about. Obviously 'justice' is a good thing. Obviously criminals are 'guilty'. No matter how far back you try to go, you always start from some obvious or natural way of looking at the situation.

three fallacies

We have never really bothered about the first, or perception, stage of thinking, because our thinking system has been based on three fallacies:

1. That the established way of looking at the situation is the only possible way, because it is right.
2. That by working logically on the situation you can arrive at the best perception of it.
3. That it does not matter where you start, because if your logic or mathematics are good enough you will eventually reach the right answer.

computer paradox

Computers are the most logical of all machines. The paradox is that it was the logical computer itself which exposed the three fallacies given above. With computers it does make a tremendous difference what concept package you choose. If the choice of package is wrong the answer may be impossible. Even if the answer is eventually reached with one package, it may take you twenty-five times as long as with another. Moreover, the computer can turn up a 'right' answer which, to everyone's surprise, fails to work in practice. It turns out that the answer is indeed right, but only in terms of the starting concept package. A computer worked out the cost benefits of different sites proposed for London's third airport and chose one of them. But this 'right' answer was unworkable because the concept package had not included the concept 'environment', and the public outcry over unnecessary noise pollution eventually forced the choice of an entirely different site. Thus the computer has shown up as fallacies the three assumptions which indicated that the first stage could be ignored if the second-stage processing was good enough. At the end of his life the great philosopher Bertrand Russell had come to precisely this conclusion. What mattered most were the concepts you set out with in the first place, and the excellence of the processing thereafter could only bring you back to these initial concepts.

computer takeover

Just as the camera took over the function of art to paint lifelike pictures, so the computer is gradually taking over the second-stage thinking process for which we developed our YES/NO thinking system. All you have to do is give the computer a concept package and instructions on what to do, and it finds the right answer to that package. Two very important points arise from this :

1. We must stop thinking that the infallible logic of the computer produces 'right' answers. This is a residue of the old idea that logic produces right answers. Neither logic nor computers produce right answers; they only produce answers consistent with the initial concept package.
2. Since computers can now take over the second-stage thinking process, we had better start developing thinking tools for the first stage, as the thinking tools we have are useless for this purpose. The huge logical efficiency of computers is wasted unless we can develop better tools for setting up concept packages. This is why I suggested at the beginning of the book that the word PO, which would at the moment be third in importance to YES and NO, will eventually become more important than either when computers have taken over more of human thinking.

PO and the first stage

The new word PO is designed directly as a thinking tool for the perception stage of thinking. PO works in a way that is quite different from the YES/NO system. The YES/NO system always requires some fixed package to work upon. PO does not. PO is designed to deal with ways of looking at things and with changing these ways to find better ones. PO has a creative function, not a judgement function like the YES/NO system. PO is used to alter and change concept packages, not to process them.

The Brain and Thinking

natural activity

Thinking is the natural activity of the brain, just as looking is the natural activity of the eyes and hearing the natural activity of the ears. The structure of the eye determines how we see, the structure of the ear determines how we hear, and the structure of the brain determines how we think.

no knowledge

It is unfair to criticize the YES/NO thinking system developed by the ancient Greek philosophers, for they had no knowledge of the brain or of how information systems work. Among other things, they considered that hysteria was due to the womb wandering all round the body. But today we have a very much greater knowledge of the structure and function of nervous systems like the brain. We also have a much greater knowledge of the behaviour of information systems. This new knowledge has arisen from our experience with computers and our appreciation of cybernetics. Far more important philosophical work arises today from computer scientists than from traditional philosophers. We have only just entered the cybernetic age and have only just begun to think in terms of total system behaviour instead of the traditional analytical process in which wholes were divided up into tiny parts for examination. Through cybernetics we are now beginning to understand patterning systems such as the brain, and the next big breakthrough in computer design will be the making of true patterning computers. So we have a fantastic advantage over the ancient Greek philosophers. That is why it is so tragic that we are doing so little to improve our thinking system but are content to let it remain as before. I refer here not to mathematics, which we have developed in a wonderful manner, but to ordinary thinking systems as applied to human affairs, and especially the first-stage thinking for which mathematics is useless.

horse and motorcycle

A horse and a motorcycle at first seem to be very similar systems. Both are used for getting from place to place. You sit astride both of them and steer both of them by pulling the front end from side to side. But you would not get very far by whipping a motorcycle that had run out of petrol or pouring petrol into a horse that was exhausted. To use a system effectively you need to know something about the nature of the system. But you do not need to know all the details. Few motorcyclists know all about the physical chemistry of petrol combustion. Few jockeys know about the role of respiratory enzymes. What you need to know are the broad characteristics of the system.

the brain system

We know quite a lot about how nerves function and how nerve networks behave. It is true that we do not yet know all the details, and it may be a very long time before we do. But, just as with a horse and a motorcycle, it is enough to know the broad type of system involved in order to be able to use it more effectively. You cannot imagine every motorcyclist or jockey sitting on the ground because he did not know all possible detail about the system he was using. But we behave in precisely that ridiculous manner with the brain. We refuse to consider the relevance of the nature of the system to our thinking behaviour until we have proved every last detail of the system. What are we waiting for? We already know enough about the broad type of information system operating in the brain to make use of that knowledge in developing new thinking tools. In fact, we have always acted on the belief that the brain functions as one type of information system. Only now the evidence suggests that this was quite the wrong system. It is not so much a matter of developing new ideas of how the brain operates as mind, but of getting rid of some of the old ideas.

Two Systems

organization

Those who wish to find out how the organization of the brain could give rise directly to what we call mind should read *The Mechanism of Mind* (Cape, 1969). In that book I discuss how nerve networks operate to give the behaviour we consider uniquely human – including creativity, humour, etc. I do not intend to repeat that material here. I only want to indicate here the very fundamental difference between two types of information system and then go on to show how this affects our thinking and our choice of thinking tools. I especially want to show why the type of system that seems to be operating in the brain demands a thinking tool such as PO.

the towel system

A towel is spread out flat on a table, and a small bowl of ink is placed nearby. A spoonful of ink is taken from the bowl and poured onto the surface of the towel at a certain place. This spoonful of ink represents the 'information input' which can be specified by reference to coordinates taken along the edge of the towel. (In other words, a unique piece of information reaches a unique place on the towel.) The information input is recorded as an inkstain on the towel. A number of different inputs are made one after the other, and at the end the towel comes to bear a number of inkstains. Since the ink is immediately absorbed by the towel, the stain remains exactly where the ink was placed. So at the end the towel bears an accurate record of all that has happened to it.

accurate memory

The towel system is the sort of accurate memory system that one uses in a computer. Incoming information is stored exactly and without alteration. It is kept permanently in this unaltered state. A separate processor then uses this stored information as it wishes, just as someone might count the number of stains on the towel, measure the distances between them, or link up some of them to form a picture. The essential point is that there is an accurate recording system and an outside processor who uses it. This is our traditional view of the brain. And it is from this view that we have developed the YES/NO system.

the jelly system

In this system the towel is replaced by a large shallow dish of ordinary jelly or gelatine which has set. This time the bowl of ink is heated by being placed in a pan of boiling water. When a spoonful of this hot ink is poured onto the surface of the jelly at some place, the hot ink starts to melt the jelly. But as the ink cools down it stops melting the jelly. When the cooled ink and melted jelly are then poured off (or sucked up) there is left in the smooth surface of the jelly a shallow depression which is the record of where the ink was placed. This depression corresponds to the inkstain in the towel system.

channels

If succeeding spoonfuls of ink are poured onto widely separated spots of the jelly surface, the final result is very much like the towel model. But if the spots are not separate but overlap, then something very different happens. If a new spoonful overlaps an existing depression, then the ink flows into that depression, making it even deeper and leaving a much smaller depression than usual at the actual spot it was placed. So at the end, instead of having a number of separate depressions, one has a sort of channel sculpted into the surface of the jelly just as a river sculpts itself into the land. Incoming ink now flows along the channel instead of remaining where it was placed.

movement, change, processing

In the towel system the ink remains exactly where it has been placed, so there must be an accurate record of what has happened to the surface – that is, the 'experience' of the surface. But with the jelly system a spoonful placed at one spot can flow down a channel and end up at a completely different place, just as if it had been put there to begin with. Thus an information input of one sort is moved by the surface to give a different sort of input. This changing of information is processing, or 'thinking'.

no outside processor

The very important point is that the towel system is a good recording system and so requires an outside processor to make something of the recorded information. But the jelly system is a bad recording system, because it alters the incoming information. Because the surface itself alters the incoming information there is no need for an outside processor.

self-organizing

The jelly surface does not actually organize the incoming information. All it does is provide a surface on which the incoming information can organize itself into a pattern. The information that comes in first alters the surface so that future information is received in a different way. The incoming information thus organizes itself into patterns.

patterns

A pattern is any situation in which you move from one state to another in a pre-set manner. Thus the channels on the jelly surface form a pattern, since ink flowing down the channel moves from one spot to another in a pre-set and predictable manner.

nerve networks

In the brain the recording surface is not jelly but a network of interconnected nerve fibres. Incoming information alters the connections in a way which makes them react differently to future information. In this way patterns are set up.

The Sequence Trap

the sequence of events

In the towel system it does not matter at all in what order the different inkstains are put onto the surface. The end result is always the same whatever sequence is used. But in the jelly system the sequence makes a huge difference. In fact, the sequence in which different spoonfuls of ink are poured onto the surface

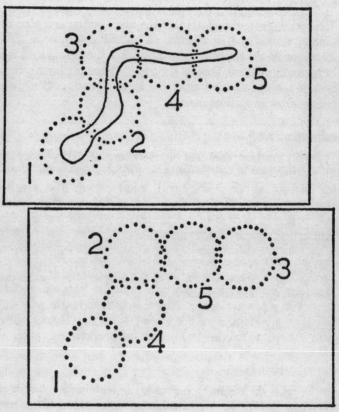

Figure 1

is as important as where the spoonfuls are poured. It is the sequence that determines in which direction the eventual channel will flow – or whether any channel forms at all. Figure 1 shows how exactly the same five spoonfuls of ink placed on the surface in one sequence give a very definite channel but in another sequence give no channel at all.

the sequence of experience

In your own personal life things happen one after another. You acquire experience piece by piece. And the particular sequence in which experience is acquired makes a huge difference to the ideas and attitudes you hold. If you were rich and then lost all your money in the Great Depression, your attitude would be quite different from what it would have been if you went through the Depression and then became rich shortly afterwards. If you marry one woman and then fall in love with another it is obviously quite different from what it would have been if you had met the second woman first. In the same way as an individual has a sequence of experience, so a culture also has a sequence of experience which makes up its history and determines its ideas. (For instance, the historical sequence of slavery determines ideas about the Negro in America.) In science the particular sequence in which discoveries are made also determines the ideas that are held. All human experience is sequential, whether it is personal, cultural, political, religious, or scientific. There may be times when a lot of new information comes in all at once, but this does not prevent further information from arriving later. Any system which exists over a period of time and is open to new experience has a sequential input of information.

make the best of it

At each moment you have to make the best of whatever information or experience is available at that moment. You cannot tell what is coming next or when it is coming. If action is required, you cannot wait indefinitely for the next lot of experience before deciding what to do. Even if you do wait, whatever experience you have up to date has already been arranged in some sort of idea.

simple model with plastic pieces

Figure 2A shows what happens when some plastic pieces are given in a certain sequence to a person who is asked to arrange them so as to give the simplest possible shape. The first two pieces are

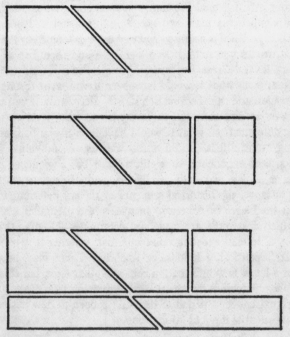

Figure 2A

immediately arranged to form a rectangle. The next piece to arrive is simply added to the existing rectangle to give a longer rectangle, as shown. But the next two pieces cause a lot of trouble, because it seems impossible to arrange all the pieces to give a simple shape.

escape from the sequence trap

The sequence in which the plastic pieces have arrived has determined the way they are arranged. You build on existing arrange-

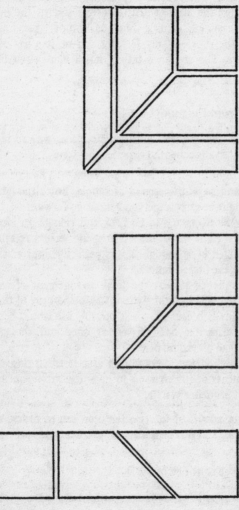

Figure 2B

ments and go on building on these in a continuous fashion. But with the plastic pieces it is possible to make progress only by going back and re-examining the long rectangle (Figure 2B). Though this was a very good arrangement at the time, you find that another arrangement is possible – a square. Once you have restructured the arrangement to give a square, the next stage is absurdly easy. I have used this model on over two hundred occasions in the course of my lectures and no one has ever reached the square. The sequence trap is much more powerful than we realize.

lessons from the model

From this simple model with plastic pieces we can learn lessons that apply to all sequential experience systems.

1. Being right at each stage is not enough. The first rectangle is right and so is the second rectangle. But although you have been right at each stage you cannot go forwards.
2. It may be necessary to go back and change an idea that was perfectly right in its time. Thus, the second rectangle has to be changed even though it was perfectly right as the development of the first rectangle.
3. In a sequence system the final arrangement of available information is very unlikely to make the best use of that information. This is because the best possible use would be made if all the information had arrived at once and the sequence of arrival had played no part.
4. Some method for re-examining and restructuring existing arrangements of information to give new arrangements is essential in a sequence system.

For 'arrangements of information' you can of course read 'ideas' or 'concept', and for 'information' you can read 'experience'.

being right is not enough

One of the major rules of traditional thinking is that you have only to be right at each stage and you can keep going forwards.

(This is the very basis of Greek/Renaissance thinking.) In any system in which information comes in piece by piece this rule is just nonsense. It is because we cling to this rule that we have so much difficulty in changing obsolete ideas and in solving social problems.

change an idea that was right

According to traditional thinking and the YES/NO system an idea is either right or it is wrong. If it is right it is absolutely right and can never need changing, and if it needs changing it cannot really have been right in the first place. Again this is just nonsense in a sequence system. In such a system an idea may be perfectly right at the time, but one may still have to go back and change it when more experience becomes available. Progress is not a matter of changing wrong or inadequate ideas but of changing ideas which have been perfectly right but are now obsolete. This does not mean that the ideas were never really right in the first place, because on any criterion they were right. It simply means that there is no such thing as absolute rightness. Any idea, no matter how right, may need changing. If this is so, then any idea, no matter how right, should be re-examined from time to time.

unlikely to make the best possible use

The sequence trap makes it impossible to use available information in the best way. That is why all sequence systems (and this includes all human-experience systems) require creativity. Creativity is precisely the process by which we escape from the sequence trap in order to look at things in a new and better way.

tools for change

Because we have always looked at the mind as a 'towel' system we have never paid enough attention to the sequence trap and other defects that are characteristic of the 'jelly' system. Thus we have developed the YES/NO system, which is designed to preserve the ideas set up by a particular sequence of experience, but have not developed any tools for creative escape from the sequence trap. PO is designed to fill this need by providing a deliberate change tool to bring about creativity.

horseless carriage

In the days of horse-drawn carriages the driver indicated which way he was about to turn by holding out his whip. So for a long time cars were given illuminated mechanical arms that flipped out from the side of the vehicle to indicate which way the driver was about to turn. It was only much later that these were replaced by the obvious simplicity of a flashing light. In the early days both electric- and steam-driven cars reached a high state of development. In fact, at one time the world speed record was held by an electric car. Had the concern with pollution from car fumes come at that time, there would be no such pollution today. But the sequence was different, and so work on electric and steam cars stopped.

crime and punishment

In the beginning of our culture and for a long time the law of man was very similar to the law of God. Breaking the law of God was sinning. The essence of religion was that a sinner was responsible and guilty and ought to be punished. Naturally this attitude was used directly with criminals who broke the law of man. This is the background to our thinking on crime and punishment. Even if we go in the opposite direction and say that it is not the criminal but his social background that is guilty we are trapped by the same basic ideas. But if we escape from the idea of guilt, then we can treat criminals not as sinners but as social inconveniences. We could also treat them as different rather than as responsible. They would be removed from society not as punishment but simply because the fabric of society could not cope with them. But they could be placed in very pleasant surroundings without any element of punishment and kept there for a long time. Alternatively, habitual criminals might be given a pension, which might be cheaper than having to protect against them, catch them, try them, and imprison them. Under the old idea of guilt such a pension would be unthinkable, because it would seem to be a reward for sin. Again, a pension might be given to prisoners who had spent so long in prison that further crime was their only way to earn a living. Furthermore, if one can get away from the idea of crime as sin, then one can start using direct reconditioning psychological techniques to make criminals better members of society. Or even chemical or surgical techniques to achieve the same end. No one would tolerate alteration on a man's personality or brain as a punishment, but if it was aid requested by him to help him live in society it would be a different matter. After all, patients are always asking psychiatrists to help them in precisely this way. At the moment, because our ideas are dominated by 'sin', we want to keep the criminal's personality intact in order to 'teach him a lesson'.

government

Our ideas on government are also very much determined by our cultural history. The demands of organization in a community required a leader. This leader was originally there by force, as in the animal kingdom, but eventually came to his position by inheritance or some variation of divine right. Since this could produce bad leaders as well as good, the principle of a changeable leader evolved. This meant that people chose a leader and then delegated to that leader their powers of choice and decision. So now individuals no longer decided about policy but about people. And that, of course, has serious limitations, as we know – the two main limitations being the practical frequency with which leaders can be changed (you may be stuck with him for many years) and the difference between personal charm and real ability. There is also the point that today government is so incredibly complex that someone like the President of the United States is in an impossible position for one man. Today we could break free from this cultural sequence trap because our technology and our interests have changed. For instance, we could have an instant voting system whereby every month anyone who was concerned about an issue could register his vote by telephone direct to a computer. With sophisticated statistical sampling techniques it might require only a very small number voting, and if the decision was so clear that it fell outside the margin of error of the method it could be taken as representative of the wishes of all the people. Perhaps we are moving slowly towards that with the growing habit of taking opinion polls on issues. But perhaps voting itself is rather antiquated and we should move more towards trend analysis. Or we could even have exams for politicians to see who was the most capable and the most aware of the wishes of the people. Or perhaps we could permit alternative societies living in parallel and in harmony, each with its own rules, laws and taxes, and a person could choose to belong to whichever one suited him best.

PO *and discontinuity*

The sequence of experience builds up ideas which are then preserved by continuity. PO serves as a tool to introduce discontinuity. We need such a tool in order to help us look for new ideas, not because we have proved the old ideas wrong but because we are aware of the sequence trap.

The Open Block

nothing in the way

When we think of a block we think of there being something in the way. But there is another sort of block, which occurs precisely because there is nothing in the way. This sort of block is just as characteristic of patterning systems as is the sequence trap we have just considered. Ink flowing along a channel on the surface of the jelly has to flow along the deep channel. It cannot suddenly decide to flow up a shallower channel which branches off the deep channel. This process is suggested in Figure 3, where the width of the path is equivalent to the depth of the jelly channel and likewise represents the degree of establishment of that path. Because the wide path is available, one is 'blocked' from

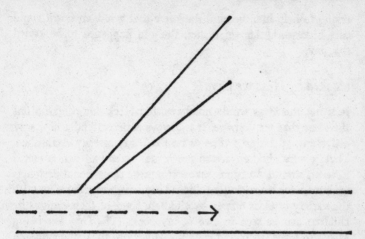

Figure 3

taking the other path. This is what is meant by the 'open block' or being blocked by openness. In real life it simply means that where there is a well-established idea or way of looking at things it is extremely difficult to find an alternative way even if one is already available.

gun behind the bar

A man walked into a bar and asked for a glass of water. The girl behind the bar suddenly pulled out a gun and shot him dead. Why? The reader is asked to offer a reasonable explanation for the strange happening. All sorts of suggestions are made: she recognized him as a dangerous criminal on the run; she thought he was about to attack her; she misheard what he said; asking for a glass of water had a special code meaning to her; and so on. All these explanations assume that the gun is used deliberately to harm the man, because that is the obvious use of a gun. It is very easy to be blocked by this obvious idea. In fact the explanation is that the man had a bad attack of hiccups, which is why he asked for a glass of water. The girl behind the bar was actually

65

trying to help him, because she knew that a sudden fright could cure hiccups. Unknown to her, the gun happened to be loaded that day.

blocked by ideas we have

It is not the ideas we do not have that block our thinking but the ideas that we do have. It is always easier to find a new way of looking at things if there is no fixed way already established. That is why children are so much more creative than adults. I have on several occasions asked groups of professional designers to draw a dog-exercising machine. They have never come up with the variety of ideas offered by children. Some of these designs by children can be seen in two of my books (*The Dog Exercising Machine*, Cape, 1970, and Penguin Education, 1971, and *Children Solve Problems*, Allen Lane The Penguin Press, 1972, and Penguin Education, 1972).

intelligence and education

Education thrives on tests and measurement. We have a fixed idea of something called 'intelligence' which we believe to be the most important mental quality. Intelligence is what makes children good at passing school exams. Intelligence is what makes children good at the IQ tests we have devised to test intelligence. But we are so blocked by this concept of intelligence that we cannot see that it may not be all that important outside the closed requirements of the education system. For instance, there is another ability which one might call 'thinking ability' (TA). In my experience, thinking ability is certainly not the same as intelligence. I have found many academically brilliant people who had high intelligence but low thinking ability. On one occasion I carried out some thinking exercises on a group all of whom had IQs of 148, which is very high. The results were no different from those obtained with other groups of much more humble IQ. I have also come across people of average intelligence who have developed high thinking ability. Other concepts which might be as important in education as intelligence or even more important are 'learning ability', 'effectiveness', 'drive and motivation'. The isolated and worshipped concept of intelligence blocks many educators from seeing the importance of other factors. It also blocks the development of newer concepts like thinking ability.

free food

The idea of 'money' is another concept that blocks the way to finding better systems for transferring goods. For instance, there could be community food stores and anyone living in that community would take as much food as he needed and then simply insert his community identity card into the machine at the check-out counter. The price is then averaged monthly over all the community residents and added to local taxes. Anyone who abuses the system may have his card withdrawn.

transport

In considering an urban bus system it is easy to be blocked by the idea that what is sold is transport. This block makes it difficult to devise a system in which not transport but comfort is sold. Basic transport is entirely free, but you pay for whatever degree of comfort you desire. So there could be open-platform buses with no charge but with a high-priced section for those who wanted to buy the comfort of seats.

money

In considering money it is easy to be blocked by the central concept that the face value does not change. If we move away from this concept and acknowledge that the use value changes considerably we might come up with the idea of dated currency, for instance a 1973 pound and a 1975 pound. The exchange rate between the two would be controlled centrally by the government and adjusted as necessary. For instance the exchange rate between a 1973 and a 1975 pound might be such that a 1973 pound would buy £1.18 of a 1975 pound. The exchange rate would take into account inflation, the state of the economy and various other factors. All wages and pensions and savings would change with the exchange rate.

perfection

It is easy to be blocked by the concept of 'perfection'. Often the expense of moving from ninety per cent perfection to one hundred per cent perfection is huge. If we look at the administration of justice we find a system which is striving for perfection. The result is an elaborate system with numerous avenues of appeal so that the chance of injustice is removed. The effect is to clog the whole system and slow down justice to the point where the delay itself becomes a considerable injustice. We could try to simplify the system with methods for quick justice and quick sentencing. To lessen the danger of mistakes there could be a system of accumulated sentences so that the first sentence was rather small but the second much bigger and the third very much bigger. The chances of a mistake occurring three times in a row would be slight. Self-sentencing is another possibility, with provision for a fuller trial if requested but the danger of a larger sentence. Road traffic would be accident-free if the top speed limit were ten miles an hour. But we adopt the more practical speed of seventy miles an hour even though this does give a definite accident risk. So instead of 'perfection' we could develop a concept of 'practical perfection'.

argument and discussion

In arguments and discussions it is very easy to get blocked by openness, for in order to communicate at all you have to use established ideas and well-recognized concepts. But, once used, these established ideas set the direction for the subsequent discussion. As suggested by Figure 3, the point at which you shoot past an alternative way of looking at things is very brief. The option does not stay open indefinitely.

PO *and the open block*

As we shall see later, one of the purposes of PO is to hold up the rapid progression along well-established pathways in order to provide more time in which to take the side roads. In this respect PO acts as a discontinuity device to halt the continuity of flow along established pathways.

Creative PO

Lateral Thinking

fashionable idea

It is only over the last few years that creativity has become such a fashionable idea. Even so, there are many circles, especially traditional academic circles, which still regard it with suspicion and resentment. It is in the world of science, mathematics, music, painting, sculpture, architecture, clothes, business, technology, etc., that the thirst for new ideas has developed. It has now become obvious even outside these circles that the rate of change in society is such that if we are to avoid catastrophe we mu t escape from obsolete ideas and develop new ones. For instance, the idea of war as a means for settling differences is recognized as obsolete by almost everyone.

creativity is haphazard

Creativity is no luxury. The individual and collective mind of man acts as a patterning system which creates ideas out of experience. Once created, these ideas become ever more firmly established and control the way we can look at present situations or new experience. Ideas are the spectacles through which we look at events in order to see information. The huge effectiveness of the human brain arises directly from its ability to form patterns which make sense of the environment. Without such pattern-making ability language would be impossible. Yet all patterning systems demand a method for breaking out of an established pattern in order to see things in a different way.

Without such a method there can only be continuity of the old ideas which become more and more obsolete. That is why progress is due to creativity which provides such a means for looking at things in different ways. But creativity is a haphazard process, and we simply wait for unusual events or unusual minds to stimulate new ideas. We rely on this passive waiting because we have never developed creativity as part of our thinking system but instead have put all our efforts into developing the YES/NO system which is essentially so anti-creative. The PO concept is a deliberate attempt to reverse this trend by providing a focus for developing creative habits.

creativity is too vague

While everyone acknowledges the necessity for creativity, it is much too vague a concept to be of practical use. That is why I invented the new term *lateral thinking*, which is a deliberate process. There are two definite reasons behind this invention:

1. Creativity is too wide a concept which applies to everything from Beethoven composing his Fifth Symphony to the man who discovered how to put a stripe into toothpaste.
2. Creativity is the description of a result after it has come about.

creativity and art

Creativity has always had strong connections with art because in the past creativity has been allowed only in the field of art. Artistic creativity involves several interacting factors: craftsmanship, talent for expression, sensitivity, emotional resonance, soul, egomania, and many other qualities. All this is quite apart from the ability to generate new ideas. In fact, in my experience several very good artists are not especially good at generating new ideas. Lateral thinking, on the other hand, is very specifically concerned with generating new ideas. There is about artistic creativity a semi-mystical flavour, because so many factors are involved that it is more a gift than a skill. But lateral thinking is a process that can be learned as a skill.

creativity is the description of a result

If you look at something and find that it is both new and effective, you say that creativity has been involved. So the process is judged by looking at the result. But exactly the same process may give no creative result on other occasions. It was a high fever that caused Alfred Wallace to come up with the idea of evolution in parallel to Darwin, who had taken twenty years to mature the idea. But thousands of other people have had high fevers without producing any new ideas. Results can be admired, and one admires creative results. But examination of a result tells us little about the process involved, for the result may be due to fever, chance, special knowledge, coincidence, etc. In contrast, lateral thinking is a process that can be used. The intention is to produce creative results, but even when such a result does not come about you are nevertheless still using the process. Whereas creativity as a result can only be admired, lateral thinking as a process can be learned, practised, and used.

lateral and vertical thinking

The word *lateral* implies moving sideways from established ways of looking at things to find new ways. This moving sideways is a search not for the best way but for alternative ways. Traditional logical thinking is 'vertical' in nature because it takes ready-made ideas and builds on them. Lateral thinking is not for building on ideas but for restructuring them. Whereas traditional thinking is concerned only with the second, or processing, stage of thinking, lateral thinking is concerned with the perception stage.

PO system and lateral thinking

NO is the basic tool of the YES/NO system, and the process of using it is called logical thinking. PO is the basic tool of the PO system, and the process of using it is called lateral thinking.

PO *and de-patterning*

The brain works to set up perceptual patterns or ways of looking at things. Our YES/NO system works to prove, establish, and preserve these patterns. The PO system works to break out of these patterns and to move laterally to find newer and better ones.

Current Pattern

current way of looking at things

The whole complex of established attitudes, concepts, feelings, values, and perceptions make up the current way of looking at things (current pattern). This current way of looking at things is established by culture, by personal experience, and by the influence of education and other people. It is often not easy to define the current way of looking at things, but nevertheless it is something very definite and it completely controls any thinking you are going to do about the situation. The current way of looking at things may be the only one you can think of or it may be the one you have chosen from among many others. Or it may be that the current way of looking at things is the only one possible with the available concepts.

jealous brothers

A French farmer is trying to divide up his land among his three sons, each of whom is jealous of the others. The task is a difficult one, because some of the land is vineyard, some woodland, and some pasture, and it is difficult to assess the relative value of each. After trying for a long time with different calculations and lines of division on the map, the old man escapes from his current way of looking at things. He tells the eldest son to take whatever portion he likes and the second son to do likewise. The third son will then choose which of the created portions he wants. In this way the responsibility for a fair division rests directly with the first son and then the second son, and if the division is unfair they themselves suffer.

promotion

The current way of looking at promotion is that a person who works hard and shows ability will in the course of his life be promoted to more and more senior positions, and with each promotion will come an increase in income. It is also understood that a person will be interested in progressing through the hierarchy in this manner in order to acquire personal achievement and status as well as income. From the point of view of the organization there is selection of a man who has shown ability in his present position and is therefore likely to manage his new position. In terms of the concept package, promotion involves position, responsibility, reward, hierarchy, seniority, ability, ambition, status, etc.

PO *and promotion*

PO can be used to break out of this current way of looking at promotion. The different specific ways in which PO can be used are described later. For the moment PO is simply an invitation to break out of the established pattern. A start can be made by separating movement, position, pay, and ability. Promotion often means that a person who shows ability in one position is removed from that position and put in a more senior one where his ability is lost. A brilliant teacher becomes an administrative headmaster and does no more teaching. A brilliant researcher becomes head of the research laboratory and has no more time for research, since he is too busy trying to find grants. A nurse who is very good with patients gets promoted and has nothing more to do with patients. A brilliant salesman who is good at selling gets put in charge of the marketing department and fails at organizing. Nevertheless, with the present promotion system such people have to try and rise in the hierarchy, since this is the only way to get a higher income to meet their increasing commitments. For the same reason a man rises through the hierarchy not for love of the job but because it is the only way he can show achievement to himself. Instead of all this there could be a system in which people stayed at the same jobs but got paid more according to ability, hard work, seniority, financial need, or any other factor. For instance, salary might increase during the period when a man had a family to educate and then decrease again afterwards. A person could also make progress without changing his position, by reducing the amount of time he had to spend doing the job, and eventually he might be working only two days a week. In this new system senior management would be a job like any other, with no more salary than anyone else. People who had managerial ability and who enjoyed doing this could enter such a position directly instead of having to work their way up through the organization and reach their position only when they were older and had run out of ideas and energy. Such a system may or may not be better than the current system, but once you have broken away from the current pattern it becomes easier to explore new ideas and move on from ideas that are at first more new than good to ideas that are both new and better than the old ones.

no loss

When you move more laterally away from current patterns, the ideas you find may or may not be better. If they are not better you can always return to the current pattern. At worst you have lost a little thinking time. But even if you have not gained a new idea, you have gained a better appreciation of the value of the old idea, which is no longer held simply because you had never considered any alternative but because it is better than the alternatives.

PO and Creativity

natural creativity

There have always been creative people who have used lateral thinking to break away from established ideas. Such people have not needed to know that it was called lateral thinking, nor have they had to wait for the PO system. Paradoxically, these are precisely the people who have shown most interest in lateral thinking and the PO system. This is because more than anyone else they see the need for the PO system. They are well aware of the elusive quality of creativity and the need for creative tools. They recognize that you cannot be creative just by willing it. They recognize above all the sheer impossibility of getting other people to be creative through exhortation. Such creative people have felt all along that creativity is based on a system that is very different from the YES/NO system, and that is why they appreciate the PO system. Not surprisingly, it is the uncreative people or pseudo-creative people who feel that they can be creative within the YES/NO system and have no need for PO.

Contrast YES/NO and PO

towel and jelly

The YES/NO system is based on the towel type of information surface. Ideas are discrete and fixed, and an outside processor selects them and puts them together. The PO system is based on the jelly surface on which the information arranges itself into patterns.

first and second stage

The YES/NO system is used in the second, or processing, stage of thinking. It gets to work on the concept package of accepted ideas and processes these to give an answer. The PO system is used in the first stage, or perception stage, of thinking. It is used to move laterally from one way of looking at things to another. You use the YES/NO system after you have accepted fixed concepts and the PO system before you have found new ones.

judgement and change

The YES/NO system is a judgement system. With it you judge whether an idea fits the existing pattern of experience or not. In this way the YES/NO system acts to preserve existing patterns.

The PO system is never a judgement system but is always a change system. With it you move away from old ideas to try and find new ones. Instead of preserving existing patterns the PO system explores and creates new ones.

pigeonholes

The YES/NO system with its definite judgements sets up classifications and categories. Much use is made of fixed pigeonholes and definitions. In the YES/NO system a definition is a sort of box, and something is judged as being completely in that box or completely outside it. The PO system seeks to break down the rigidities of classifications and categories in order to look at things in different ways. In the PO system you do not use pigeonholes or boxes for definitions. Instead you use flagpoles. This is suggested in Figure 4. The upper part of the figure shows the usual box-type definition, and someone is judged as being either a friend or an enemy. In the bottom half of the figure is shown the flagpole type of definition. Here someone is nearer one pole than the other but can still be seen as related to the other pole if you choose to look at things in that way. In the YES/NO system a person must be either all friend or all enemy in the usual type of polarization, but in the PO system a person may be either without any difficulty. Thus the YES/NO system creates polarizations, but the PO system breaks them down.

single or many

The YES/NO system is worked hard in order to find the best answer. This answer is the one that is nearest to being absolutely right. Therefore any other different answers must be inferior and any contradictory answers must be wrong. In the PO system there may be many different answers all of which have their own validity.

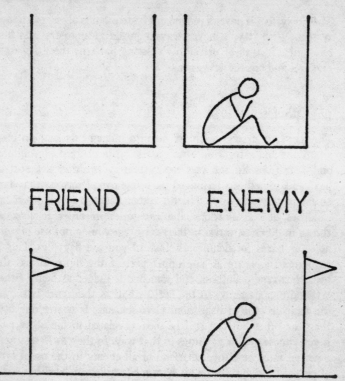

FRIEND   ENEMY

Figure 4

fundamental difference

There are many fundamental points of difference in the way the two systems operate. The two most extreme points of difference are:

1. In the YES/NO system you must be right at each step, but in the PO system being right is not important.
2. In the YES/NO system you consider only what is related to the situation, but in the PO system you can bring in random material from outside.

being right

The very essence of logical thinking is that you must be right at each step. But in the PO system you may be quite wrong at some step on the way to finding a new and effective idea. This involves the use of an 'intermediate impossible', which is a wrong idea used as a stepping-stone. The process is described later on.

random material

In the YES/NO system you concentrate on what is relevant to the situation, since you are trying to analyse the situation. But in the PO system you can bring in random material from outside and juxtapose it with the situation to see what ideas develop. This process is also described later on.

relationship of PO to the YES/NO system

Although the PO system and the YES/NO system are used in different stages of thinking, there are times when PO is used directly to counter the effects of the YES/NO system. These occasions are as follows:

1. PO is used to protect an idea from the sharp judgement of the YES/NO system so that it can act as a stepping-stone to further ideas.
2. PO is used to challenge YES/NO judgements and classifications that have been made in the past.
3. PO is used as a by-pass to ask for different ways of looking at things without having to reject the current way first.

mixture

In practice the use of the PO system is mixed in with the use of the YES/NO system. The PO system provides the creative element.

Humour

more significant than reason

Humour is a more significant process in the human mind than is reason. In practice, reason may be more useful, but as a type of process humour is more significant. Reason is a selecting process and is easily carried out by a machine, and indeed we have developed excellent computers to do just this. But humour involves a switching over from one way of looking at things to another. This is absolutely essential in a patterning system, for it is the basis of creativity, and patterning systems cannot progress without creativity.

computers cannot laugh

It would be very sinister if computers could laugh. If they could laugh they would be capable of creativity and of self. Computers cannot laugh, because they have no choice but to arrange the available information in the best possible way according to the programme they have been given. If a computer could break away from the obvious way of looking at things and find a different way of looking at them, then that would be humour. And if a computer could do this it would be creative, because it would start producing answers that went beyond the instructions given it. It would also be capable of self, because the operator would no longer be able to control or predict the computer's behaviour. It would have developed a personality of its own. Computers will be able to laugh as soon as we have developed proper-patterning computers – because humour is possible only in a self-educating patterning system. As we have seen, such systems (like the jelly system) create pattern out of experience. Humour involves switching out of the obvious pattern to use a different one. That the human mind is capable of humour is further evidence that it is a patterning system.

humour and expectation

The essence of a pattern is that it is well established and therefore predictable. If you say the word *gun* the listener has a definite expectation as to what you mean. Humour involves breaking away from the obvious expectation to find another meaning that is seen to be possible after it has been found.

salad

The simplest type of humour is to be found in children's riddles and puns: 'Why was the tomato red?' 'Because it blushed to see the salad dressing.' Or a straightforward pun:

'How do you get two elephants in a mini?'

'One in the front and one in the back.'

'How do you get two giraffes in a mini?'

'One in the front and one in the back but you have to make holes in the roof?'

'How do you get two whales in a mini?'

'Along the motorway to Bristol and then over the Severn bridge.'

Children love this one. In each case humour is obtained by switching over from the obvious meaning of a word to an alternative meaning which makes us look at the situation in a new way.

two politicians

At dinner one evening Winston Churchill was placed next to Lady Astor, who was known for her forthright views. She was angry with Mr Churchill, and, turning to him, she said, 'Mr Churchill, if I were married to you I should put poison in your coffee.' The expectation is that Mr Churchill would resent having poison put in his coffee and would therefore counter this with some awful vengenace of his own. But his reply was, 'Madam, if I were married to you, I should drink that coffee.' The move is directly contrary to expectation but very effective.

the Great Depression

At a cocktail party a man was explaining how his family lost everything it had in the American Depression 'when a man jumped out of the twentieth-floor window of a skyscraper'. The expectation is that the family had been very wealthy and that the collapse of the stock market had so ruined them that the head of the family committed suicide by jumping out of that window. The man continued his tale: 'Yes, we lost absolutely everything. You see, that man landed right on top of my father's ice-cream cart.' As before, the story breaks right away from expectation and yet makes perfect sense.

the cheapest store in town

Some people find the following story very funny, but others fail to see the point and do not find it funny at all. There were two rival stores across the main street from each other in a small town in the USA. One day one of the stores put up a sign: 'The Cheapest Store in This Street'.

'The Cheapest Store in This Town', countered the other.

'... in This Part of the Country'.

'... in This State'.

'... in the USA'.

'... in the Western Hemisphere'.

'... in the World'.

'... in the Universe'.

This seemed to be the end of the escalation, because there was no area larger than the universe. But after a short pause the first store owner simply replaced his sign: 'The Cheapest Store in This Street'.

It is the sudden switch-over to a new way of looking at things which is funny. At first both stores claimed cheapness on an absolute scale by indicating the size of the area in which they were cheapest. When one of them had come up with an apparently unbeatable claim on this basis the other one suddenly switched over to realizing that all he had to claim was being cheaper than his rival no matter what the rival claimed.

humour and the PO system

Humour belongs directly to the PO system.

Insight

humour and insight

In humour there is a switch-over from the obvious way of looking at things to another way which is just plausible. We can see that the new way is possible, but it really is not very likely. So from a practical point of view humour is not very constructive though it can still be useful in easing rigid views and fierce situations. Insight is exactly the same process as humour, but with insight the switch-over is to a new way of looking at things that is much better than the original way. In my lectures I often give the audience problems which seem quite complicated. And then I show how with an insight switch-over the solution is obtained very easily. The audience invariably bursts out laughing even though there is nothing funny about a straightforward mathematical problem. It could be said that humour is reversible insight, since one does find a new way of looking at things but returns from it to the more practical way; or that insight is permanent humour, since you switch over to the new way and then stay there because it is so much better.

insight switch-over

Look at Figure 5. Quite obviously it consists of two rectangles which have been made to overlap, as suggested in the sequence at the bottom of the page. But if you look at the figure again you might suddenly switch over to looking at it in a different way – without any new information input. If you cannot do this, then turn to Figure 6.

three slow horses

The three cowboys were puzzled. To stop them from fighting in his saloon, the barman had offered a prize to the slowest horse in a race from one end of the main street to the saloon. All afternoon they had stood around at the end of the main street arguing about the race, for each one was determined to be the last to reach the saloon. Suddenly one of the cowboys jumped on a horse and rode furiously towards the saloon. Immediately the others mounted and rode furiously after him. What had happened? The answer is simple. The first cowboy had suddenly realized that if the prize was to go to the slowest horse all he had to do was race someone else's horse to the saloon ahead of his own. The other two also made this insight switch-over in perception, and a proper race was on.

the crawling fly

Figure 7 shows an arrangement of coins. A fly lands on the coin marked 'F'. Is it possible for this fly to crawl over each coin without ever going over the same coin twice? If you wish you can try out all the different paths available to the fly in order to see if it is possible. Or you can try for an insight-type solution. For instance, instead of regarding the coins as all being equal you can put a cross on alternate coins as shown in Figure 8. There are thus thirteen crossed and twelve uncrossed coins. If the fly starts on the 'F' uncrossed coin, he has ahead of him eleven uncrossed and thirteen crossed coins. Since he can reach a crossed coin only from an uncrossed one, there are simply not enough uncrossed coins left, so the journey is impossible. This insight approach is very much simpler than trying out every possible route.

two problems

You can try out the following two problems for yourself before reading on to the answers.

1. How quickly can you add up all the numbers from 1 to 20?
2. 134 players enter for the singles section of a tennis tournament run in the usual elimination way. What is the least number of matches that must be played?

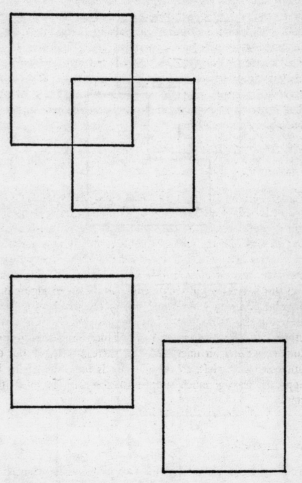

Figure 5

With each problem there is a routine approach which will certainly give an answer. But there is also an insight approach which involves switching over to a new way of looking at the situation.

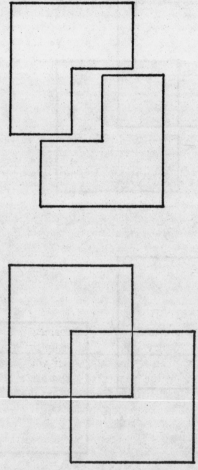

Figure 6

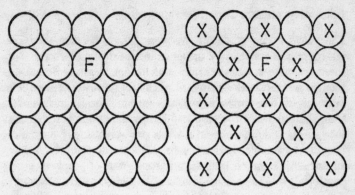

Figure 7   Figure 8

Gauss

The numbers from 1 to 20 can be added together in about three seconds. You look at them as a sort of seesaw with the middle number at 10½. You subtract ½ from the next number above, which is 11, and add it to the number below, which is 10, to give 10½ in each case. If you do this all the way up and down you will level the seesaw and have 20 x 10½, which gives 210 as an answer. This is exactly the insight which the famous mathematician Gauss used as a child, astounding his teacher with the speed at which he added the numbers together.

losers

The usual approach to the tennis-tournament problem is to lay out the pattern of play and then count up the matches required to get to the winner at the end. But if you switch over from being interested in the winner to being interested in the 133 losers, you will find that each game must have one loser and each person can be a loser only once. So the least number of matches must be 133.

take for granted

The above examples of insight were chosen because they are self-contained and clearly demonstrate the insight process. But there are more practical examples of insight ideas all around us, though we now take many of them for granted. The whole business of hire-purchase buying was an insight switch-over from the usual idea that you had to buy something before using it to the idea that you bought it while you were using it. Insurance is another example. This could be looked at as group buying in advance. For instance, in fire insurance a group of people together pay for all the fire damage that year but agree to pay before the damage has occurred. The simple idea of the supermarket is a switch-over from the old idea of shoppers being served to shoppers serving themselves. There must be many other ideas just as basic and waiting for someone to make the necessary insight switch-over to get them going.

fire on a tanker

Fire breaks out in one of the oil tanks of a tanker while at sea. The obvious thing to do would be to try to empty that tank and the adjoining tanks to prevent the fire from spreading. In fact the captain of the vessel does exactly the opposite thing: he pumps more oil into the tank and the adjoining tanks and so denies space to the explosive air/oil mixture. In hindsight this is seen to be a very good way of tackling the problem.

hindsight

In hindsight every single insight solution must be obvious. And usually it is the very obviousness of the solution that makes it so infuriating. This obviousness in hindsight but not in foresight is very characteristic of a patterning system, and it is further evidence of how the brain works as a patterning system. People who do not understand the insight process or patterning systems often declare that if a solution is obvious and logical in hindsight, then all that was needed in foresight was better logic. This claim is best answered by giving such people a simple problem. When they fail to solve it you reveal the solution, which is obvious in hindsight, and imply that if logic was sufficient they must have been very stupid not to have solved it. But of course it is not a matter of logic but of being trapped by the obvious way of looking at things. This process is shown in Figure 9. You

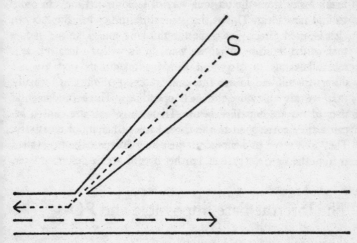

Figure 9

move along the wide track because this is the established way of looking at things, but if 'somehow' you can get to the solution, then in hindsight it is obvious how you could have got there.

PO *and insight*

Insight, like humour, belongs directly to the PO system. You cannot get to the insight solution by following along the obvious path created by experience. Nor is the YES/NO system much use, because its function is to keep you on the path created by experience. What you need is a method for 'somehow' getting to the insight solution shown in Figure 9. Once you are there, then in hindsight you can easily find the logical path. Since we have no such method, we wait for chance or inspiration to get us there.

CREATIVE PO

PO *as a specific thinking tool*

The PO system is to do with lateral thinking and creativity. As we have seen, the PO system contrasts with the YES/NO system. The word PO is the name of a system, a concept, an attitude, an indication of the patterning nature of mind, and an invitation to break away from the obvious way of looking at things in order to find new ideas. This is the general nature of PO. But PO can also be used directly as a specific thinking tool. Like NO, it is a tool which indicates what we want to do with an idea. PO as a tool allows us to carry out thinking operations that are not otherwise allowed in our thinking system. PO indicates formally that we are carrying out such operations. Three fundamental uses of PO are described below. These three uses are chosen because they correspond to the three basic principles of creativity. They also serve to demonstrate just how different the PO system is from the YES/NO system. Further uses of PO are described later.

The Intermediate Impossible and PO-1

the wheelbarrow experiment

Figure 10 shows a new design for a wheelbarrow. Examine this new design as closely as you like and then make some comments about it – preferably on a piece of paper.

Figure 10

bad design

I have used this wheelbarrow design on many occasions in my lectures to students, designers, engineers, etc. I ask them to write down their comments. The result is always the same. Everyone comments on what a bad design it is and picks out the many faults. Criticism is always twenty times as heavy as praise:

'Unstable, it would tip over if left alone.'

'More difficult to push down on the handle than to lift.'

'The wheel would tend to sink into the ground, since it is bearing twice the weight of the load.'

'The joint between handle and wheel strut is very weak.'

'The wheel is in the wrong place.'

children's view

I asked a classroom of twelve- and thirteen-year-old children to comment on the design. Some of their comments:

'Since the wheel is near your foot, you could easily kick off any mud.'

'Much easier than the usual wheelbarrow for going around sharp corners.'

'Pushing down is less likely to strain your back than lifting.'

'Easier to tip over a low wall or into the middle of a hole.'

'You could have a spring on the wheel strut and so automatically weight every load.'

Some of these ideas are not very useful, but others make very good sense. For instance, if you are wheeling a barrow along a narrow path or along planks on scaffolding it is impossible to turn a sharp corner with the conventional design, because your feet are so far from the wheel that you would have to stand in space in order to get around. So, following the child's idea, auxiliary wheels could be fitted to an ordinary barrow to give this advantage (Figure 11A). The suggestion about tipping could also be used as a stepping-stone to a new idea by putting hinged wheels under the usual barrow (Figure 11B). Finally, the spring-loaded strut could turn each barrow into a self-weighing machine (Figure 11C).

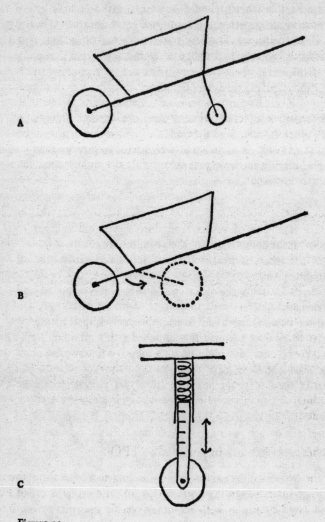

Figure 11

rejection and the YES/NO system

The most fundamental rule of the YES/NO system is that if you come to an idea that is wrong you reject it at once. The whole of our traditional thinking rests entirely on this rule. Without this rule logic would simply cease to exist.

quick to reject

Because we have all been brought up strictly according to the YES/NO system, adults reject the wheelbarrow design because it is a 'wrong idea'. In fact, many of the comments simply state, 'The wheel is in the wrong place.' Only the children adopt a more creative attitude.

critical

Most people look at a new idea only in order to see what is wrong with it and how quickly they can reject it. Engineers are always telling me that their instinct with any new idea is to find out why it is not worth considering. But this attitude is not confined to engineers. Administrators, teachers, politicians, business executives, all have the same attitude, with rare exceptions. I remember once sitting around a table with a group of very senior engineers and someone put forward a good new idea. Everyone around the table gave some reason why it would never work. Only creative people are free from this immediate-rejection instinct, although even they often apply it to someone else's work out of rivalry.

the 'intermediate impossible' and PO-1

The first use of PO as a specific thinking tool is to allow the use of an intermediate impossible. This first use of PO is called PO-1 to avoid confusion with the other specific uses of PO. An intermediate impossible is an idea that would be rejected at once in the YES/NO system. PO-1 acts to protect the idea from rejection.

stepping-stone

An intermediate impossible is an idea that is wrong or impossible but nevertheless can be used as a stepping-stone to a new idea that is right. Thus we see that the impossible design for the wheelbarrow could be used as a stepping-stone to new ideas that made sense. The use of an intermediate impossible is completely contrary to logical thinking in which you have to be right at each step. That is why we need a device like PO to indicate what is happening.

what happens

When you use an intermediate impossible, three different things can happen:

1. Instead of rejecting the idea at once you look at it a bit longer and find good points that you would never have noticed had you rejected it right away.
2. Judged within the framework of your current views on the subject, the idea may be wrong ('the wheel is in the wrong place'). But if you hang on to the idea you may find that it is right and that your current framework may need changing.
3. The idea is definitely wrong and will always be wrong, and yet it can act as a stepping-stone to new ideas that are right.

outrageous ideas

The intermediate impossible is useful with ideas that at first seem wrong but later turn out to be right. Since virtually all new ideas must at first be judged wrong – because they cannot fit the old framework – this function of PO is very useful. Nevertheless PO-1 can also be used with ideas that are completely outrageous and will always be wrong. That is why PO-1 is so much stronger than the word *suppose*, which offers weak support to ideas that are likely but not actually proven. PO-1 can use as a stepping-stone not only unlikely ideas but also impossible ones: 'PO motor cars should have square wheels.'

why PO-1 works

Figure 12 shows a modification of the patterning-system diagram we have come across before. You move ahead along the well-established pathway and miss the side turning. But if 'somehow' you could get to the solution, then in hindsight it is seen to make good sense. PO-1 is a tool to get to that solution, for it provides a means to jump over the NO barrier. Once the solution is reached, the justification does not depend on the NO pathway.

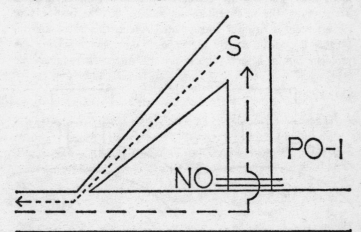

Figure 12

river pollution

Industrial pollution of rivers is a very serious problem. What happens is that a factory puts out polluted water into the river and it is the people downstream who suffer. To help solve this problem you could set up the intermediate impossible: 'PO the factory should be downstream of itself.' This is clearly an impossibility, because the factory cannot be in two places at once. It cannot be upstream and at the same time downstream of itself. Yet this intermediate impossible can be used as a stepping-stone to a simple idea that does make sense. To make a factory downstream of itself you have only to switch over the inlet and outlet pipes to the river and insist that the inlet pipe must be downstream of the outlet pipe (as shown in Figure 13). The factory is now the first to be aware of its own pollution.

urban street cleaning

Most streets in a town tend to be dirty. The town dwellers complain about inadequate street cleaning, but the sanitation department insists that the dirty streets are the fault of the inhabitants. You can try the intermediate impossible: 'PO the best way to clean streets is to dirty them more.' Again, this seems absurd, because it goes in exactly the opposite direction to solving the problem. But, as before, you can use this intermediate impossible

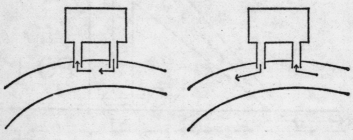

Figure 13

as a stepping-stone to an idea that does make sense. Periodically the local authorities (or the inhabitants) scatter tiny discs of coloured paper in the streets. A record is made of the date on which a certain colour is used. In this way you can tell directly from the length of time the discs remain on the street how efficient the cleaning has been. With this as an indicator it becomes possible to contract out street cleaning to private agencies whose efficiency can now be judged.

parking

As the number of cars increases, parking becomes a problem in most towns. The usual way to control parking is to try and discourage it with meters and no-parking areas. But you could use an intermediate impossible here: 'PO drivers should be encouraged to park in towns.' This is again exactly contrary to the established way of looking at things, but from it you can go to an idea that does make sense. This is the idea of parking discs labelled with a day of the week (Monday disc, Tuesday disc) and the vehicle registration number. Each driver could get only one of these discs. The disc allows the car to be parked anywhere in the town on the specified day without payment of any meter charge or fine. In this way you spread the shopping load throughout the week instead of having it bunched together at a peak period. You also give commuters some incentive to use each other's car, for five neighbours could get together and use only one car a day, with the appropriate disc.

when to use an intermediate impossible

There are three different occasions on which an intermediate impossible can be used:

1. In your own thinking when you come to a wrong idea that you would normally throw out at once. Instead you protect it for a while with PO-1 and see if you can use it as a stepping-stone to other ideas.
2. When other people come to you with an idea that you could reject at once. Instead you use PO-1 and listen and see where the idea can take you.
3. You can deliberately set up an intermediate impossible in order to solve a problem which requires creativity.

setting up an intermediate impossible

This is done by turning an idea upside down, inside out, back to front, and so on. You can reverse a situation, exaggerate it or distort it. You say the most unlikely and outrageous thing you can about the situation – and then see where it gets you. For instance, if you were setting up an intermediate impossible to generate ideas on supermarkets you might come up with:

PO all food should be free.
PO there should be no choice at all.
PO they should get up and come to your front door.
PO the cashiers should make deliberate mistakes in charging.
PO different prices should be charged to different people.
PO all the food ought to be chained to the shelves.

Each of these statements is outrageous and impossible in terms of current supermarket practice, but each one can be used as a stepping-stone to a useful idea.

attitude and tool

PO-1 and the intermediate impossible can be used deliberately as a problem-solving tool. But even if you are never likely to be concerned with problem-solving, PO-1 can still be used as an attitude. The attitude is simply that of stopping yourself from rejecting new ideas that you feel able to reject at once. Instead you look at them more closely, either to find value in them somewhere or to use them as stepping-stones to other ideas. This applies both to your own ideas and to the ideas of others. For instance, you may be inclined to reject the PO concept because by definition it does not fit in with the YES/NO system to which you are more used. Instead you say 'PO' to yourself and see where the idea can take you.

first principle of creativity

PO-1 corresponds directly to the first basic principle of creativity. The first basic principle of creativity is the overcoming of the NO barrier so that ideas can be used as stepping-stones to other ideas. This is a very fundamental point indeed, because our whole intellectual culture is based on esteem of the critical intelligence and we need some way of countering this in order to be able to explore and create.

Random Juxtaposition and PO-2

concentrate on what is relevant

In our traditional thinking system, when you are examining a situation you concentrate on what is relevant and keep out what is irrelevant. This is because traditional thinking requires a well-defined situation, which is then analysed. Unless you draw the boundaries of this situation in a definite manner, analysis is impossible. For instance, if you are considering education, then you concentrate on such relevant factors as schools, teachers, children, books, teaching machines, exams, curriculum, subjects, financial support, etc. You would certainly not include in your analysis carrots, neon lights or bottles, because if you did you might as well include everything you can think of, and that would make analysis impossible.

juxtaposition in art

In our traditional YES/NO thinking system we put things together because there is a reason for putting them together. The reason is that in our experience they fit together (school and teacher) or have simply occurred together (two books were left on the table). In the world of art, however, it is quite common to put together things which have no reason at all for being put together. Once they have been put together the juxtaposition provokes new ideas and it is these new ideas that justify it. For instance, a modern piece of sculpture might consist of a frying pan with some butterflies in it. This arrangement is not an advertisement for delicate cooking or instructions for frying butterflies. But from the juxtaposition come ideas of beauty, fragility, and the ephemeral contrasting with durability, solidity, and usefulness. One viewer may go away with a feeling of the need to balance both ingredients in his life. Another viewer may be excited to start looking again at ordinary things like frying pans to find their natural beauty.

poetry

In prose you follow the YES/NO system and put words and images together because there is a reason for doing so. But poetry belongs to the PO system, and here you put words and images together in order to achieve a stimulating effect. The effect occurs only after the juxtaposition has been tried and not before.

only from within

If you look at a situation only from within your established way of looking at it, no amount of will power is going to take you to a new way of looking at it. You draw the boundary and work within that boundary, and your answer will also lie within that boundary.

PO-2 and random juxtaposition

The second use of PO as a deliberate thinking tool is to enable you to create new juxtapositions which have not occurred in experience and which are unlikely to occur. This use of PO is called PO-2 to distinguish it from the other uses. The purpose of the new juxtaposition is to create a new experience that can set off new ideas. For instance, you can put together the idea of 'education' with the idea of 'neon light'. There is no reason for putting these two ideas together, because the second idea was picked at random out of a dictionary. PO simply serves to keep the two ideas together in one context.

truly random

When you have exhausted the different ways of looking at the problem from within, you bring in this random word in order to generate a fresh approach. The word that comes from outside is truly random and is not selected for its relevance to the problem. Nor do you take one random word after another until you find one you like, because that is also a form of selection.

link up

With practice and confidence you can always generate ideas out of a random juxtaposition no matter how remote the word may at first seem. The connection may be direct or indirect, but this does not matter, for the purpose is simply to stimulate ideas, not to prove a point. For instance, if the situation is 'noise pollution' and the random word is *anthracite* you might connect them as follows:

Anthracite comes from underground, perhaps we ought to try to keep all traffic underground in cities.

Perhaps if you really wanted quiet you should live underground. Special quiet underground rooms could be provided in towns for relaxation and escape from noise pollution.

Anthracite is black, which suggests dark and night, but there is no darkness for sounds. We do not have earflaps to shut off sound the way eyelids shut out light. Perhaps we could develop such flaps or train ourselves in self-hypnosis to shut out noise.

Anthracite is dirty because of the black dust, which rubs off. Perhaps we ought to clean up all the incidental noise that is not essential to function. Train people as noise scrubbers.

why PO-2 works

There are so many ideas stored away in everyone's brain that if you start two ideas going from separate points they will eventually link up. The purpose of bringing in a random word from outside is to provide a new entry point. If we return to the pattern diagram shown in Figure 14, we see that we are looking for ways of breaking out of the established path in order to reach the solution which, once reached, is obvious in hindsight. PO-2 and random juxtaposition simply provide a different starting point outside the established pathway.

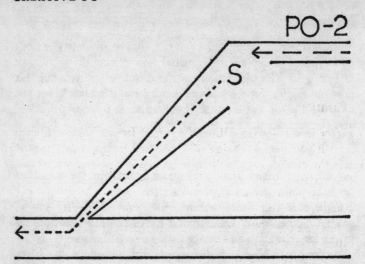

Figure 14

a new confectionery

The problem is to design a new type of confectionery. The random word is *telephone*, so the juxtaposition is: 'Confectionery PO telephone.' Not a very likely juxtaposition, it would seem, and yet it is possible to generate ideas:

Telephones have dials so that you can select whom you want. What about dialled confectionery? For instance, a coin-operated machine in which you could dial different tastes and textures and the result would come out as a sort of rope of intertwined strands. Or you could have little globules, each with a different taste or texture and each coloured differently. You could then mix the globules as in a cocktail to get whatever taste you wanted – e.g. nut and crunch with chocolate, or lemon and peppermint chew.

Perhaps a candy which made noises or buzzed as you ate it, in order to provide more sensation. Perhaps a vibrating cigarette for those who wanted to give up smoking but still required oral stimulation.

Telephone delays. A confectionery with delayed tastes so that the taste would change two or three times as you ate.

A hand-held device which squirted small jets of confectionery into your mouth.

education

Earlier in this section I listed the sort of factors you would consider if you were analysing education and then went on to suggest the random juxtaposition 'Education PO neon lights'. From this juxtaposition you do not simply proceed to discuss the merits of neon lighting in schools but generate other ideas, like the following:

Just as neon lights are part of the environment, perhaps education should be more part of the environment. Why should children have to go to special places at special times in order to be educated? Perhaps there could be street screens with loop projectors, or even just street speakers.

Neon lights suggest advertising. Advertising has built up a huge expertise in communicating ideas effectively. Education should make use of this expertise much more fully. (The American TV show *Sesame Street* is a start in this direction.)

Perhaps there could be an education tax on advertising – for instance, ten per cent of all bought advertising space or time to be used for educational purposes. This could mean either one advertisement in ten to be educational or a strip one tenth of the advertisement size or one tenth of the effort of an advertising agency (and paid for by the manufacturer).

Neon lights and entertainment. More research on the psychology and methods of entertainment. Why shouldn't education be entirely entertainment?

Night life and entertainment. Perhaps disco-schools which mix dancing and lessons. Learn together as a couple.

Circular neon-light systems suggest a circular education system in which students become teachers for the students just behind them and so knowledge flows on in a stream. In order to teach the material the students have to learn it better themselves. Examine not the students but their pupils.

politicians

Most people have definite ideas about politicians. We can see what happens if we try the random juxtaposition 'Politicians PO bottles'.

Empty vessels make the most noise. Perhaps research to see whether noise is related to useful work, and an index on each politician to give his 'noise' level.

Bottles can be corked. Perhaps a politician-free holiday for three months every year when all the media omit to mention politicians.

Useless when empty. Politicians continue in power even when drained of ideas. Perhaps a sort of citizens' jury which examines politicians in public for their idea content at election time.

The opposite point of view to the preceding one. Perhaps politicians should be empty bottles and then be filled by the desires of the people they represent. Politicians would be professionals like actors and would carry out whatever role was assigned to them. They would only have to be skilled operators and would not be expected to be personally consistent or involved or contribute anything other than political skill. They would simply provide channels through which the people could make their wishes felt. They would be hired and fired for their efficiency, not because they had pretty faces and the current issues at heart.

The label must match the content of a bottle. Perhaps in place of a voting system each competing politician would be given a list of current issues and asked to estimate the response of the electors to those issues. A poll would then be carried out on these issues, and the politician whose guess was closest to the actual poll result would be chosen automatically.

There is a refund when some bottles are returned. Each politician could be given a fund at the beginning of his term of office, and if he did not perform satisfactorily he would have to return all or part of the fund at the end. Thus there would be a positive incentive to work harder and a man would not be in power simply because his electors did not like the other party.

A bottle can be used to fill up with fluid or for pouring fluid out of. How much is a politician a receiver of views and how much a generator of views? Perhaps there is a need for two separate sorts of politician – the true representatives of the people's wishes and also the leaders who try to lead the people forward. There could be one chamber for legislative innovation and then another chamber as a sort of jury to accept or reject the ideas put forward. Perhaps it is too much to expect that the true representatives of the people can be progressive leaders.

words, things, and people

So far we have used words for the random juxtaposition. Such words can be obtained from a dictionary, using a table of random numbers or by opening it by chance at any page or in any other way so long as you do not deliberately select the word. Or you can create a list of about fifty special words and then use one of these. To begin with, the best words are simple familiar words you know so well that it is easy to generate ideas: soap, nose, shoe, egg, umbrella, window, cup, beer, etc. Though words provide the most convenient 'packaging' for ideas, you may also use things to provide the random juxtaposition. For instance, when I am asked to invent something I go off to the nearest chain store and pick up something at random and so create a juxtaposition with the problem that is in my mind. Or you may go to an exhibition that has nothing to do with your direct field of interest or talk to someone from an entirely different background. The main point is that you are bringing in something from outside and are not selecting that thing for its relevance to the problem.

PO-2 as attitude

You may not be much involved in direct problem-solving. Nevertheless PO-2, like PO-1, can be used as an attitude as well as a specific thinking tool. The attitude is one of being open to outside influences and of seeking out such influences. Instead of shutting yourself away and believing that problems can be solved simply by concentrating on them, you open yourself up to outside influences and see how they can help you. The main point is that you cannot look at something in a new way simply by looking harder at it in the old way.

basic principle of creativity

PO-2 corresponds exactly to the second basic principle of creativity. The second basic principle of creativity involves opening yourself up to influences which have no connection with what you are doing. New experiences create new ideas. Instead of waiting for the rare new experiences to happen we create them deliberately in our mind.

Challenge for Change and PO-3

the rejection mode

In our traditional thinking system, if you hold an idea that is right you do not go looking for other ideas. Nor do you change the idea until someone has proved it to be so wrong that you reject it. In the YES/NO system an idea must be wrong before it is changed, and an idea must be rejected before you can move to an alternative idea. This 'rejection mode' is the way to change ideas.

by-pass

If you ask someone a question and he offers you an answer, the only way to get a different answer is to reject the first one. It is only if you reject the first way of looking at things that you will get another way. Having to go through this 'rejection mode' in order to get new ideas is extremely inefficient, for three reasons:

1. There may not yet be enough evidence to reject the old idea.
2. The person defending the old idea may hang on to it even when there is enough evidence to reject it.

3. When you have rejected the original idea you will have nothing to come back to if you do not find a better one.

In short, if you have to go through the rejection mode, then changing an idea takes a great deal of time and a great deal of effort. The third use of PO as a specific thinking tool is to provide a 'by-pass' to the rejection mode of the YES/NO system.

change without rejection

This third use of PO can be called PO-3 to distinguish it from the other uses already described. As before, PO is never a judgement, for it works outside the YES/NO judgement system. When an idea is challenged with PO it does not mean that the idea is right or wrong or even that it needs changing. PO simply acts as a by-pass to the usual judgement and asks for a change without having to go through the rejection mode.

put it on one side

What PO-3 implies is indicated by the following sentences.

'That idea is fine, but let us put it on one side and find a new way of looking at things.'

'That is one way of looking at things and it is perfectly valid, but it does not exclude other ways, so let us try to find some.'

'I wonder if there are other ways of looking at this.'

So you put the original idea on one side, without rejecting it, and start looking for other ideas. In this way you can start exploring at once. Moreover, if the alternative ideas you discover are not much use you can go back and use the original idea with an enhanced view of its value. In the old YES/NO system you would probably still have been attacking the old idea in order to destroy it before you could even start looking for new ideas.

alternatives

PO-3 is simply an invitation to generate alternative ways of looking at situations.

no concept graveyard

The older a culture gets, the more does it become cluttered with concepts, since it is easy for a concept to come into being but very difficult for obsolete concepts to die. We badly need a concept graveyard. As explained earlier, obsolete concepts provide 'open blocks' because they make it impossible for us to look at things in a new way. We cannot destroy these concepts, because they are too intertwined with the very fabric of our culture. That is why we need PO-3 to act as a by-pass to allow us to step past these concepts to find new ways of looking at things.

why PO-3 works

The familiar pattern diagram is shown in Figure 15. As we have seen, PO-1 and PO-2 are thinking tools to help us get to the insight solution which is obvious once we have got there. The function of PO-3 is temporarily to block the open pathway or established way of looking at things so that we can deliberately step sideways to look for an alternative pathway as shown in Figure 15.

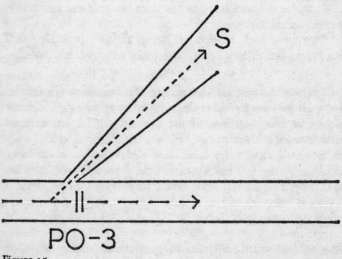

Figure 15

PO-3 *as focus*

PO-3 can be used in a general way to by-pass an established idea, but it can also be used to focus dissatisfaction on a particular concept. Thus with the statement 'Urban transportation is impossible because everyone wants to go to work at the same time,' you could challenge the whole statement with PO-3 or else focus PO-3 and say 'PO time'. From this you might go on to the idea of there being alternative clock systems and different people living in a different clock system with friends, work, etc., in that system (Time-A, Time B, Time C).

concept package

As we have seen, the YES/NO system is used after a concept package has been accepted. The logic of the YES/NO system works faultlessly to provide a solution which is consistent with the starting package. Thus if you accept the starting concept package it will be impossible to get a different answer. But if you challenge parts of the concept package with PO, then you can start looking at things in a new way.

challenge

As before, PO does not judge whether a particular concept is right or wrong. What PO does is challenge the uniqueness of that concept, the necessity for looking at things through that concept. If you can show that the concept is not uniquely necessary, then by changing to a different concept you can come up with new answers.

why

PO-3 is a formal way of saying 'Why?' or 'Why do we have to look at things that way?' or 'Why use that concept?' In this regard PO-3 is much better than 'Why?' because the answer to 'Why?' is usually a defence of the concept, but there is no answer to PO except 'I myself cannot think of any other way to look at this.' Such an answer is very weak, because it is no longer a defence of an established view but an admission of a lack of imagination.

dogmatism and arrogance

PO-3 is a direct attack on dogmatism and arrogance. Dogmatism and arrogance both insist that the way things are being looked at is the only possible way. PO-3 is a direct attack on this supposed uniqueness.

trade unions and wages

'It is the duty of a trade union to ensure that its workers are paid a fair wage.' We could challenge every single concept in this statement in a search for new ideas. We can start at the end and challenge 'wage' and move to the idea that a company does not just pay wages but also provides health services, insurance, housing, cheap mortgages, holidays and so on. To some extent this already happens in Japan at worker level and elsewhere at executive level. Continuity need not be a problem. Next we could say 'PO fair' and perhaps move on to the idea of separating a fair wage from a living wage. Once this is done then a fair wage could be determined mathematically in relation to cost of living increases, productivity, utility, market value, etc. In some cases a fair wage would actually be lower than a living wage. Poorly paid workers who were nevertheless getting a fair wage would then have their wages increased to reach the living wage which would be determined in relation to the average wage across all industry. By challenging 'paid' we could explore the idea that wages should be given as right by the government and not the employer. The employer would then pay substantial bonuses according to the amount of work done. This would be a rationalization of the unemployment system but would also allow fuller employment because a company would not have to bear full wage costs. The concept of 'worker' could also be challenged and instead of the concept of work we could try responsibility. Work is directly related to effort but responsibility is related to participation, which may only take the form of work at times. The concept of 'its workers' is also open to challenge. Perhaps wages should not be determined piecemeal by individual unions but by an effective trade unions parliament with real power and responsibility acting across union boundaries. 'Ensure' could also be challenged because it implies continued pressure and demands and so becomes the central function of a union. Instead of such pressure to 'ensure', the unions could be put into a position of directly paying the fair wage from a total wage bill established on a contract basis with government or industry as a whole. The concept of 'trade union' is easy enough to challenge because its historical development has so determined its nature. Other bodies, organizations, methods of representation are easy to suggest. PO duty. While it remains the duty of a trade union to ensure a fair wage then the estimation of that fair wage is also the duty of the union and this may be too incestuous. Perhaps it should be the duty of society to ensure the fair wage. In none of these cases is it suggested that the alternative ideas are new or better than the existing ideas or even feasible. It is simply a matter of opening up new lines of thought for exploration in the first instance and for evaluation when a definite proposal has been arrived at.

freedom

'The organization of society must not interfere with the freedom of the individual.' A safe statement with which few would disagree. Nevertheless, we can say 'PO freedom' and see what happens. This is obviously not a matter of saying that freedom is wrong but of trying to look at freedom in a different way. We may reach the idea that 'non-interference' is a better concept than freedom, because freedom for one person to do what he likes can interfere with the freedom of other people. For instance, your freedom to play your radio loudly in the park interferes with the freedom of others to have peace. Your freedom to smoke in a cinema or to drive a car interferes with the freedom of others to breathe clean air. Freedom is an egotistical concept that is centred on the individual, whereas 'non-interference' is centred on the reaction between individuals. Perhaps non-interference is a much more practical concept, since it gets round the usual difficulty of having to decide when freedom becomes licence. A person who is not interfered with and does not interfere with others is free. But under the old concept a person who claims freedom for himself may yet interfere very much with others. Perhaps some of our social troubles arise from the obsolescence of the concept of freedom in a crowded society.

efficiency

Efficiency, like freedom, is a well-established concept that is one of the pillars of our society. Nevertheless, let us say 'PO efficiency'. Efficiency means that there is some work to be done and the less we pay to get that work done the more efficiency there is. Efficiency is the exchange rate between cost and product. Thus industry can no longer afford to employ people at the required wage because they cannot provide a value sufficiently in excess of it to give efficiency. Suppose we turn from the concept of efficiency to the concept of effectiveness. One man painting a door in two hours might be efficient, but three men painting the same door in four hours would still be effective even though not efficient. With the efficiency concept we go from money to work to paying people for doing the work. With the effectiveness concept we go from money to paying people and then to organizing work. In the efficiency system a company employs as few workers as possible in order to make profits. In the effectiveness system a company is required to employ a fixed number of people at a standard wage and then it makes its profit by organizing productive employment for them. In the effectiveness system people come before products, whereas in the efficiency system it is the other way round.

bureaucracy

'The only way to make government departments productive is to see that everyone puts in a full day's work.' We can use the PO challenge at several different points :

PO productive: Government departments are often very productive in producing a lot of useless paper and unnecessary work for themselves. Perhaps we could use the concept 'useful' instead.

PO everyone: Why not have some part-time people such as students or mothers who would be able to move in and out on unusual work schedules which fitted in with their other commitments?

PO full day: Why do people have to work a full day? Let everyone go home just as soon as he thinks he has finished his work. The responsibility is now his and there is a great incentive to cut out unnecessary work and to be efficient. And if you cut out your own work, then everyone else all down the line benefits. In fact, you might fire for inefficiency anyone who did a full day.

hold button

In computers there is sometimes a 'hold' button which allows you to hold for consideration whatever the computer has presented at that moment. Without this hold button the computer would immediately move on to something else. PO-3 acts like this hold button. PO-3 holds a concept or phrase or statement in view for further consideration so that you can look at it in different ways. Without PO-3 you tend to move on too quickly and to reach conclusions which are determined by the particular concepts you have glided over at the outset.

PO-3 *as attitude*

PO-3 can also be used simply as an attitude. The attitude is one of anti-dogmatism and anti-arrogance. The attitude implies that a way of looking at things may be perfectly right but does not exclude other points of view. The attitude implies that the conclusion you reach with so much certainty is really determined by the concepts you have chosen at the beginning. The attitude

113

implies a willingness to look again at concepts no matter how well established.

basic principle of creativity

PO-3 corresponds directly to the third principle of creativity. The third basic principle of creativity is the willingness to look again at ideas which seem perfectly right and absolute.

General PO

The General Use of PO

de-patterning

The three uses of PO as a direct thinking tool (PO-1, PO-2, PO-3) were each a special application of the general nature of PO. As we have seen, the general nature of PO is to provide a means for escaping from the patterns set up by experience. These patterns decide the way we look at things, and PO is designed to provide a device for looking at things in a new way. So the basic function of PO which underlies all its various uses is one of de-patterning.

discontinuity

The mind always continues in its established way of looking at things or dealing with them. In providing a means for escaping from this established pattern, PO provides a device for introducing discontinuity. Continuity is the basic feature of a patterning system like the mind. You look at things in the way you always have done, you carry out the same actions and reactions that you always have done. PO is a discontinuity device which allows you to break away and do things or look at things in a new way.

many situations

As we shall see, there are many situations where we badly need a method for breaking continuity. This is what PO is designed for, since our usual thinking system only emphasizes continuity and provides no means at all for breaking it. These situations require the general use of PO as a discontinuity or de-patterning device, in contrast to the specific creative uses described previously. Nevertheless, this general use of PO is just as definite and deliberate.

PO as Release

fixed ideas

One major type of mental illness consists in a person having a fixed view of the world which does not correspond with reality (as determined by others), cannot be changed by experience, and makes life difficult for that person. An extreme and obvious example is paranoia, when a person believes that he is being persecuted. Whatever happens to him or around him is taken as being evidence for this persecution. If someone treats him kindly, then the paranoiac looks with suspicion for some ulterior motive in this kindness. Another obvious example is phobia. One person may be terrified at the thought of going out into the street and so spend years shut away inside a house. Another person may be terrified of heights, or open spaces, or closed spaces. Like paranoia, these phobias are fixed. A person who is afraid of heights will be genuinely terrified if placed on top of a high building. Moreover, his fear will get worse and worse, because not only is he afraid of heights but he will come to be afraid of his fear of heights.

complexes and hang-ups

Paranoia and phobias are extreme cases of fixed ideas, and they are relatively rare. Complexes, hang-ups, neuroses are less extreme and far more common. In each case there is a fixed way of looking at the world or some part of it. This way has been established by a sequence of experience or even a single experience. The main point is that through continuity the hang-up or complex becomes ever more firmly established. This is because a person with a particular way of looking at the world will find that his view of the world reinforces that fixed idea. Thus, a man who is terrified of being impotent will in fact find that he becomes impotent. A woman who believes that men are interested only in sex will find that men are interested only in sex. By this process of selection and exaggeration it is possible to support any fixed way of looking at the world. The whole process is one of myth-making. A myth is a fixed way of looking at the world which cannot be destroyed because, looked at through the myth, all evidence supports that myth. Any fixed idea may seem nonsense to someone outside it, but that does absolutely nothing to alter the complete truth of that point of view to the person inside it.

up-tight

On a still more common level than complexes and neuroses are individual situations where you get caught up in the continuity of the thing and become up-tight. There are many personal situations where you get trapped by your way of looking at things and are so convinced that this is the only possible way that you get frantic. Most problems are created not by circumstances but by a particular perception of them.

release

When people have built up a fixed way of looking at the world that is oppressive, dull, or hopeless, they often find their escape in alcohol, drugs, or frustrated violence. More acceptable ways are meditation and mysticism. All these are escape methods for getting away from a fixed view of life and the world. Since society has never developed or approved of any escape methods other than religion or psychiatry, these various instant escape methods increase in popularity as the complexity and pressures of society increase.

discontinuity and by-pass

The essence of a fixed idea is continuity. It grows on itself. The man who is afraid of heights becomes afraid of his fear of heights. For the woman who spends years locked away in a house the outside world grows more and more terrifying. The man with a hang-up finds that he gets into situations that exacerbate and reinforce that hang-up. As a discontinuity device, PO serves to break into this vicious circle at an early stage. PO does not attempt to destroy a fixed idea but accepts it as one way of looking at things and then puts it on the side in order to find another way. PO challenges not truth but uniqueness and dogmatism. PO allows you to accept the hang-up but by-pass it instead of letting it dominate your life.

instant meditation

In a way this escape use of PO is like instant meditation or mysticism. When you are in an up-tight situation you say 'PO' to yourself to indicate that the way you are looking at the situation is not the only way and if you can step aside from it you can break the continuity. PO is a reminder that your fixed perception may actually be creating the problem. Like meditation, PO releases the mind to achieve a new perspective. With practice in this use PO can become a sort of tranquillizer. But the effectiveness depends entirely on the amount of practice you invest.

complexity

Sometimes the trouble is not a single fixed idea that makes life difficult but a general feeling of confusion and pressure as things around build up to an unsupportable degree. At this point some people achieve discontinuity by simply walking away. But this is rather extreme, and you cannot keep walking all the time. Complexity usually arises; you start off with a way of looking at the situation and then get carried along into complexity because you are unable to change the fixed way of looking at things with which you started (e.g. that infidelity means your husband no longer cares for you). Once again the problem is one of continuity. You can use PO in this situation to put on one side the complex view of things and start again with a newer and simpler way. With PO you do not have to prove the old way wrong or the new way better. You simply by-pass the old way and start afresh.

fogweed

In certain areas such as philosophy and even religion immense complexity comes about because philosophy always builds on existing ideas which there is no way of dropping. Thus people torture themselves with complexity and questions and inadequacy as they struggle to cope with an exceedingly elaborate way of looking at things. Academics even feel that complexity is a virtue in itself. 'Fogweed' is a special intellectual weed which grows very abundantly in intellectual circles but serves only to obscure and never to reveal. It is often impossible to fight your way through the fogweed to discover the real basic issue. Since we have no way of killing the obsolete ideas that give rise to the fogweed, PO can be used as a weed-killer to cut through the continuity that gives rise to this sort of complexity. As before, PO is used to put the complex view on one side and to find a newer and simpler approach.

PO and Obsolete Ideas

concept prisons

It is very difficult to get rid of concept prisons which have been perfectly valid in their time but are now inadequate and even dangerous. Even when such concepts are harmless in themselves they can still block the way to the evolution of better concepts. It is usually very difficult to prove such concepts wrong, because they have become so much a part of culture that they are supported by surrounding concepts. For instance, the concept of 'capital' is so intertwined with the concepts of 'ownership', 'profit', 'investment', and 'inheritance' that they all support each other as a fixed way of looking at productivity. You cannot drop 'profit', because it is supported by the concept 'investment' in so far as there would be no investment without profit. If we have to wait until a concept is proved inadequate before we try to change it, then it might be too late because there is no alternative concept available.

PO *escape*

With PO you do not have to destroy concepts, but you escape from concept prisons in order to look for new concepts. For instance, it has taken us much too long to develop the concept of 'environment' as an actual entity and not just the space between other entities. We have not yet begun to develop the concept of 'happiness' as a skill that can be learned in education. Nor have we developed the concept of 'life style' as something that can be designed much as a living room is designed. We have not yet exchanged 'expansion' for 'stability'. We still hang on to 'success and failure' instead of using a new concept of 'development' which relates what is happening to what could be happening (fulfilling potential). The ancient concepts of 'cause and effect', which relate to a fixed universe, could be replaced by 'change and communication', which make it possible to start thinking in system terms. Another obsolete concept is 'revolution'.

PO and Revolution

clash

The concept of revolution is based directly on the YES/NO system. On the one hand there is the solidity of the establishment, made even more solid by the attacks on it. On the other hand there are the revolutionaries, who accept the solidity of the establishment and therefore the need to attack and destroy it before change can take place. Conservative and revolutionary both fit exactly into the same NOPO mould of mind. Both believe their ideas are right and beyond change. It is merely a matter of swapping one idea for another. The arrogance of the left wing is matched by the arrogance of the right wing. Because revolutionaries are also brought up in the YES/NO system they disconnect themselves from what is to be changed and then try to destroy it from outside or to build up an alternative system to replace it. The paradox is that even those who are attacking the rigidity of the establishment crave that same rigidity themselves. To attack something rigid, even with no hope of success, gives as definite a form and purpose to your life as belonging to the rigid system.

disconnection and discontinuity

There is a huge difference between disconnection and discontinuity. Discontinuity means escaping from the momentum of the past and moving in a new direction. Disconnection means destroying the vehicle and using a new vehicle which may end up going in the same direction as the old one.

discontinuity and chaos

Discontinuity is not chaos but a change in direction. If you were to change direction at every pace, then you would have a random walk that began to resemble chaos, as shown in Figure 16. But a simple change in direction is different, as shown in the bottom part of Figure 16.

PO as slogan

PO is for discontinuity, not disconnection. PO is a slogan for new ideas and change but not for clash and confrontation. PO is for evolution rather than revolution. Instead of the standard sequence of polarization, opposition, and clash, PO is for developing new alternatives and new methods for change. PO is not for formless wishy-washy liberalism, but for effective development and new patterns. It is not a matter of destroying old patterns so much as of being able to switch over to new and better patterns which in their turn will eventually be exchanged for even newer ones.

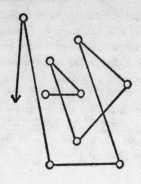

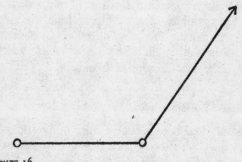

Figure 16

order and stability

PO is anti-arrogance, anti-dogmatism, anti-rigidity, and anti-polarization. But all that does not make PO in any way anti-order or anti-stability. On the contrary, PO is for stability and order, because it seeks to provide a better tool for changing ideas than the very disruptive clash method of the YES/NO system. PO accepts the validity of different points of view but opposes the attempt to force the rightness of your point of view on others. PO is in favour of alternative points of view and of people doing their own thing, but PO is against being so trapped by that point of view that you are unable to consider or explore others. PO accepts that everyone is right but that no one is right enough to be rigid.

tool for change

PO is not change. Nor is PO for change. PO is simply a tool for change. You may have a change tool and never use it, just as you may never have enough confidence to use the reverse gear in your car. You may choose to drive round by a very circuitous route, but someone else may get there much more quickly by using the reverse gear.

three structures

Figure 17 shows three types of structure. The small circles represent people. The first is the skeletal type of structure in which each person has a fixed position and cannot move. The second type of structure consists of a series of interconnected envelopes. Within each envelope people may move freely provided they do not overstep the boundary. If a person wants a different set of boundaries, he can move to a different envelope. In the third structure instead of boundaries there are totem poles representing different interests and aspirations. A person is free to position himself between poles, to stand as near or as far from a pole as he wishes, to oscillate from one pole to another, or just to keep moving. The first type of structure is the rigid YES/NO structure. The second type of structure is governed by YES/NO boundaries but is very much freer than the first type. The third is a PO structure.

Cool PO

immediate reaction

A friend of mine was driving abroad when he saw by the roadside an injured woman who appeared to have been knocked down by a car. He stopped and got out to help the woman.

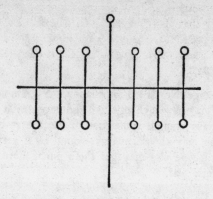

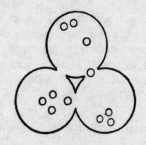

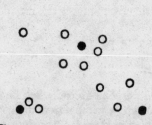

Figure 17

At this point another car drew up and the occupant got out and hit him so hard that his jaw was broken. The driver of the second car had recognized him as a foreigner and jumped to the conclusion that this foreigner, driving with typical carelessness, had injured the woman.

pause

There are times when the obvious way of looking at things leads to an immediate reaction. There are times when an automatic reaction has become so established for certain situations that no thinking is involved. For instance, if someone swears at you the reaction is to swear back. PO can be used in this sort of situation to interrupt the continuity. PO acts as a neutral pause to be placed between obvious perception and automatic reaction. The purpose of this discontinuity is to allow you to move to a reaction that is better than the obvious and immediate one.

escalation

Escalation is a double version of the above situation. Someone does something to you and you react; he then reacts to your reaction, and the escalation accelerates. For instance, in Northern Ireland the police were keeping order after civil-rights demonstrations; the Catholic population reacted to the reaction of the police, so troops were brought in; then the IRA came in as a reaction to the troops, so more troops were brought in and internment was put into force. Escalation in riot situations as in personal situations is often inevitable. To stop the escalation it is necessary to break the continuity of the situation. For instance, in a riot situation withdrawal of the police may de-fuse things. PO acts as a crystallization of this 'cool-it' attitude. It introduces discontinuity in order to prevent over-reaction and escalation. As usual, the purpose of PO is de-patterning. We very much need such a deliberate de-escalation device, because otherwise both parties get trapped in the continuity of a situation neither really desires. The original situation is soon forgotten as you react not to it but to the reaction of the other person. PO acts as a sort of mental or internal shrug. Eventually actually saying 'PO' can come to have this cooling effect when the concept is widely understood.

PO and Conflict

arguments

In the YES/NO system, if you are right the person who holds a view opposite to yours clearly must be wrong. So you have a duty to point out to him how right you are and how wrong he is. Likewise, he sees his duty as requiring him to do the same to you. So an argument develops to see who is right and who is wrong. There is nothing in the YES/NO system to indicate that both sides may be right but simply starting from different basic ideas or different ways of looking at things.

quarrels

One husband who had left a book of mine lying around was very disconcerted when his wife took to stopping quarrels simply by saying 'PO'. Used in this way, what PO meant was 'Let's agree to differ – let's accept that we are looking at things from a different point of view.' It is quite true that in ordinary quarrels you may eventually reach this conclusion at the very end of the quarrel. But with PO you can start out at this point and then spend the time examining the different starting positions. This applies not only to quarrels but to any argument situation.

humour

PO can serve as humour does, to introduce discontinuity into a situation that has grown unnecessarily solemn, self-important, or fierce.

PO and Discussion

explore

The introduction of PO and the PO attitude into a discussion indicates in a formal manner that you are more interested in exploring the matter than in proving that you are right. By using PO you indicate that you want to go beyond the YES/NO system in order to turn up new ideas and new ways of looking at things. Once you have introduced PO, then flexibility, movement, and alternatives become more important than certainty and being right all the time.

change ideas

In the course of a PO discussion you may come across a new way of looking at things that is so much better than your old way that you switch over to it at once. But even if you do not reach the point of this insight switch-over, the PO exploration remains valuable because the mind cannot make disappear an idea to which it has once been exposed. So the ideas that you develop in the discussion remain around and may in future come together to give you the new idea that eludes you at the moment. In addition, the use of PO lessens the rigidity of the ideas you do hold, so that when it becomes necessary to change them you will find it much easier to do so.

PO and Uncertainty

doubt

Because PO is directed to turning up new ideas and to seeing different points of view, there might seem to be a danger that it would weaken action and decision, for these are best based on fanatical certainty no matter how misplaced.

effectiveness

The ultimate aim of the PO system is exactly the same as that of the YES/NO system – effectiveness. With the PO system you open up new approaches and create new ideas in order to reach a solution that is clearly better than any other solution. If one of the alternatives you turn up is not obviously better than the current way of looking at things, you are left with a number of new alternative ideas. You can then examine these alternatives in the usual way to see which one fits the situation best. This suggestion may upset those people who find that the best way to make decisions is to have no alternatives at all. Such people do object that the creativity of PO makes their work harder. But even such people can adopt the simple rule that if none of the alternatives turned up by PO is obviously better than the original idea, you return to that idea without having to examine each alternative in detail.

retardant doubt

In the YES/NO system you require the certainty that you are right before you can act. In a decision you have to know that the alternative you choose is absolutely right. If you do not have such certainty, your doubt retards and holds you back. What usually happens is that to overcome this doubt you create a false certainty which gives rise to a lot of trouble later because you do not realize how false it is.

propellant doubt

In the PO system there is no certainty. There is only an acceptance that the current way of looking at things is the best one at the moment but may need changing very soon. This means that instead of hanging back and waiting for complete certainty you can act without it. That is why this sort of doubt is called 'propellant' doubt, because it propels you forward to action. You act in a pragmatic way knowing that your action is not right in any absolute sense, but for that reason you are all the more ready to change it as soon as circumstances demand. Far from paralysing by indecision, the PO system actually speeds up decision by allowing you to deal with uncertain situations much more effectively than in the YES/NO system.

uncertainty

The YES/NO system cannot deal with vagueness, uncertainty, and insecurity, because you cannot make a definite judgement about something that is not itself definite. That is why people, companies, and governments which all work exclusively within the YES/NO system feel so lost when so much of modern life is uncertain on account of the fast rate of change which prevents tomorrow from being a repetition of yesterday. With the PO system you do not rely on the certainty of fixed situations. Instead you explore the situation in a wide-ranging creative way and then find an effective idea and use it – but with the willingness to change it for an even better one. Instead of requiring certainty to give you confidence in action, you build up confidence from the wide-ranging exploration of alternatives and the knowledge that you can change your approach as soon as it is necessary to do so without stubbornly trying to defend or justify it.

PO and NO

Judgement is the basic function of logical thinking and NO is the tool used to carry it out. Movement is the basic function of lateral thinking and PO is the tool used to carry it out.

Why We Need PO

PO *and patterns*

We need PO because the mind sets up fixed patterns which determine the way we can look at things and this is not always the best way. So we need a de-patterning device like PO to enable us to move laterally to find better ways. We call this process creativity.

already

Having read so far, some people will find that they already have all the PO attitudes. Others may find that many of the PO attitudes are now evolving in modern society, especially among the young. The most honest will find that they already have some of the PO attitudes and find the remainder easy to accept. Why, then, do we need PO itself? It may be suggested that those who accept the PO attitudes do not need PO itself and that those who do not accept the attitudes will not be persuaded by PO.

focus

PO serves to focus creativity. Natural creativity is an urge that is ill-defined and vague. Usually it is no stronger than a dissatisfaction with things as they are and the feeling that somehow they should be changed for the better. It is very difficult to apply this vague feeling in a deliberate or practical manner. That is why PO is necessary as a focusing device.

attitudes

It is much easier to claim a creative attitude than to use it. That is why PO as a crystallization of a set of attitudes provides a means for applying those attitudes in a definite manner.

specific tool

It is no more possible to be creative through will power than it is possible to hoist yourself into the air by standing in a bucket and tugging upwards on the handle. To develop creative skill you need specific tools with which to practise. The specific uses of PO provide just such tools.

problem-solving

In addition to providing creative tools for practising the creative attitudes, PO tools can be used for direct problem-solving by those who are not interested in the PO attitudes.

skill

Many people do develop a creative skill in one particular situation but find it difficult to transfer this creative skill to other situations. This is because skills are so complex that they become attached to the particular setting in which they have been developed. The best way to transfer skills is to embody them in a tool. So you develop skill in the use of PO as a tool and then this tool can be transferred to any new situation carrying the creative skill with it.

counterbalance to YES/NO system

The YES/NO system is a well-defined system which our culture has developed as its basic thinking method. You cannot counterbalance such a definite and well-established system with the vague idea that 'creativity is a good thing'. You need to show that creativity is based on an alternative system which is just as definite but very different. This is the PO system. It is by showing the difference between the two systems that you can lessen the rigid hold of the YES/NO system and demonstrate that it is not the whole of thinking. It is not enough to complain that the YES/NO system is too rigid and that creative flexibility would be nice. This is mere sentiment and of no use from a practical or educational point of view.

medieval devil

The medieval clerics made the natural urges of the body into sins such as gluttony and lust. In a parallel way PO turns into sins the natural rigidity and arrogance of the mind. Once you are aware of these sins it becomes easier to avoid them. But PO is more practical than the medieval clerics because it offers a direct opportunity for escaping from such attitudes – not just the threat of punishment.

exhortation is useless

It is unfortunately impossible to make other people creative by exhortation, example, or trying to transfer your own creative urge. But a tool such as PO can be transferred and the method of using it taught directly. PO provides a tangible means for developing creativity in others.

teachable

The word NO, disapproval and a smack are a natural part of child-rearing if only because homes are so full of things that are dangerous to a child or just breakable. Later on YES and NO form the basic reward system in school. It is against this background that a child develops the use of YES and NO as tools for thinking. It is hardly surprising that they come to be used with dogmatism, rigidity, and emotion, since they have been founded on emotion. If we made a deliberate effort to introduce PO along with NO at an early age we might not only build up an escape mechanism from the fierceness of YES/NO but also an attitude of creativity and exploration. As a child grows up and learns all the right answers his opportunities for interest and exploration diminish. The PO habit acquired at an early age can serve to make life more interesting. PO, creativity and lateral thinking can also be taught directly at school in order to counterbalance the formal rigidity (see *Lateral Thinking: A Textbook of Creativity*, published by Ward Lock Educational).

talkable

Because PO acts as a crystallization of the creative attitude, it makes it possible to talk about the attitude in a more definite way. This is difficult with a vague attitude which means different things to different people and which covers everything from artistic inspiration to rebellion. PO and the PO system are specific concepts that can be discussed and talked about whether in agreement or disagreement.

banner, slogan, symbol

The word PO becomes a banner, a slogan, and a symbol for the PO attitudes. Like all symbols, it is a brief way of stating a complex concept. Like all slogans, once it is there you can use it to effect. Like all banners, it can be held aloft to inspire other people or to indicate your discontent with things as they are.

magic word

The Hindu chant 'Om', through constant repetition, comes to act as a conditioning signal to bring about a feeling of detachment. In the same way you could condition yourself to react to PO as a tranquillizing signal for use in tense or anxious situations.

notation

In the PO system you can use words and ideas in a way which is not permitted in the usual YES/NO system. For instance, you may say, 'PO people should be cut up and the different parts transported around the town' (an intermediate impossible used as a stepping-stone to solve urban traffic problems). Or you may say, 'Political parties PO toothpaste' (a random juxtaposition to generate new ideas on political organization). In both cases PO serves simply as a notation to indicate what is happening. Without such an indication there would be confusion, for the listener would not know what you were about and would think you were mad. PO is a creative notation, just as the square-root sign is a mathematical notation.

language and PO

It might be asked why the word PO did not evolve by itself in ordinary language if it is so necessary to our thinking. The answer is that it could never evolve in ordinary language, because it is an anti-language word. Language is our strongest patterning system. We can use words only if we accept them as meaning their most obvious meaning. It is essential for communication purposes that words have a fixed meaning, and in order to make that meaning more and more specific we put words together to remove all ambiguity. The way we put words together must also fit our experience. But, as we have seen, PO is essentially a de-patterning tool. Moreover, PO allows us to break the rules of language and put together words which are not connected in any way whatsoever. We must remember that language is primarily a communication device and hence is inadequate for thinking, since thinking has different requirements – for instance, creativity. Thus PO has to be invented outside language and then added to language to make it more suitable as a thinking medium.

active PO

Active PO is for those creative people who want to find new ideas and bring about change. Active PO is for those who feel the need to escape from some of the concept prisons of the past.

passive PO

Passive PO is just as real as active PO, but it is for those who feel no urge to go out and create new ideas but just want to be able to perceive things in new ways. Passive PO is for those who, while not able to create new ideas, are able to understand, appreciate, and develop them. This is just as important a role – or, rather, more important, since the generation of ideas is less valuable than the use of them.

The Use of PO

your choice

For some readers it will be enough to classify themselves as PO people and to classify as NOPO people the rigid minds they encounter. Others will go further and understand the need for PO, its place in our thinking system, and the use of the PO attitudes. Yet others will go further than understanding and will develop the PO attitudes. Finally, there are those who will find themselves so in tune with PO that they will start using it as a basic part of their mental equipment.

general PO and specific PO

Many people may mistakenly believe that the PO system consists in the use of the specific tools PO-1, PO-2, and PO-3. This is not so at all. The purpose of these specific tools is threefold:

1. To show in a concrete manner how the PO system differs from the YES/NO system.
2. To provide specific creative tools which can be used deliberately when you want to generate new ideas about a situation.
3. As an introduction to the PO system. By practising the specific PO tools, you can build up an understanding of the PO system and the attitudes involved.

Some readers may be unable to understand the PO concept but

may find the specific tools useful in problem-solving. Others may adopt the general use of PO and the PO attitudes but find it very difficult to use the specific tools. The most important point about the PO concept is the general use of PO as a de-patterning device and as a counterbalance to YES/NO rigidity. The specific uses of PO are a minor part of this.

PO *in language and thought*

Some may be able to use PO only within their own minds and in their own thinking. Others, less timid, may want to use PO in language as soon as possible. At first it may seem awkward and artificial, but it becomes natural after a while.

grammar

There are five basic uses of PO in language :

1. In front of a word, phrase, sentence, etc., to indicate that what follows is taken as one particular way to look at things. This use includes both the intermediate impossible ('PO motor cars should have square wheels') and also the PO challenge ('PO freedom').
2. As a connector between words, phrases, or things, to indicate that a random juxtaposition is being made ('Political parties PO toothpaste').
3. On its own as an interjection. Thus, you can simply say 'PO !' in reply to a statement or assertion. You can also say it to yourself after reading an argument or in a tense situation. This use of PO simply indicates 'That is one way of looking at things, but it does not exclude others.'
4. As an adjective. This will be discussed later.
5. As a noun to refer to the PO concept or the PO system.

response to provocative PO

When someone puts forward a random juxtaposition or an intermediate impossible, the response is to try to develop ideas from it. The situation is a cooperative one, with both of you trying to use the intermediate impossible as a stepping-stone or the random juxtaposition as a new starting point.

response to PO challenge

The natural tendency is to respond to a PO challenge by defending the idea that is being challenged. This pushes you back into the YES/NO system. The proper response is to accept that your way of looking at things is just one way and not unique. You invite your challenger to develop alternative ways, and you try to help him do so. Even if neither of you is successful you can still accept that there are other ways which you have not succeeded in finding. Your lack of success does not prove the uniqueness of the idea, only your limited creativity.

response to PO shrug

When PO is used as a 'cool-it' device or shrug to interrupt the continuity of a tense situation, the proper response is to shrug back by repeating 'PO' and so allow the situation to cool.

PO as adjective

One of the easiest uses of the word PO is as an adjective. As a starting point towards the fuller use of PO, this simple use is worth practising.

PO person:	one who is in tune with PO and understands it.
NOPO person:	one who simply cannot understand PO, especially someone who is very rigid and dogmatic.
PO thinking:	exploratory and creative thinking free from ego-pushing and the need to be right all the time.
NOPO thinking:	rigid, dogmatic, up-tight, and concerned only with proving a point of view.

PO attitude: the sort of open-minded attitude outlined in this book. Relaxed but not chaotic and formless. Not pseudo-creative with all the trimmings but none of the substance.

NOPO attitude: cramped, righteous, and small-minded.

PO situation: a fluid situation capable of developing into something, a stepping-stone situation; can be applied to art, politics, etc. Also a provocative situation, provided those involved regard it as such.

NOPO situation: fixed, cut and dried, and incapable of development.

PO scene: as for PO situation, only more temporary.

NOPO scene: as for NOPO situation, only more temporary.

PO discussion: deliberately exploring, not an argument between two sides to see who is most right or most stubborn.

NOPO discussion: a clash between rigid ideas, with both sides determined to win without changing their ideas at all.

PO glass: an attitude through which you look at obvious things in an effort to look at them in a new way.

NOPO glass: concentrating on the obvious and established.

These are only some examples of the use of PO as an adjective. You can develop any other uses you like.

Deliberate PO

not easy

PO is not easy, because the natural tendency of mind is to remain within the security of the rigid patterns it has set up. So PO requires effort and practice before its use becomes a natural part of your mental equipment. But then creativity is not easy, either.

Above all, you need to make a deliberate effort to use PO, because it will not happen to you suddenly by itself. It is very hard for adults brought up on the YES/NO system to escape its constriction. Thinking habits are not changed overnight.

NOPO

attack

There are a lot of NOPO people who get very upset at the PO concept. They express their anger by attacking the concept in one of the following standard ways:

1. That it is dangerous to remove the order provided by the YES/NO system, for the result must be chaos.

   Answer: The PO system does not introduce chaos but introduces the possibility of changing the present order for a better order without having to go through the disruptive chaos that results from the clash method of change which is the only method available in the YES/NO system. Furthermore, in the past the greatest danger has arisen from the rigidity of ideas, not the absence of rigidity (e.g. Nazism, Northern Ireland, religious persecutions).

2. That PO is unnecessary because we already have tools for creativity in language and thought.

   Answer: Where are these tools? I have done a great deal of work on creativity, including experiments on some forty thousand people, and have not come across such tools. The best we have is the word *suppose*, which is an ineffectual form of just one of the many functions of PO. We do have some natural creativity, but we do not have tools to make creativity available as a skill.

3. That the PO concept is not new, since people have always held PO attitudes.

   Answer: Some of the attitudes may not be new, but PO and the PO system are new because they are a crystallization of such attitudes into a usable form. What is also new is the basis for PO as something that is demanded by the patterning behaviour of the brain. In any case, newness is not a virtue. If PO makes available in a concrete way attitudes that were not easily accessible, that is sufficient purpose.

4. That PO is an overstatement of what is needed to improve the YES/NO system.

Answer: If something needs saying, then it is best to say it in a definite manner and in a manner which makes the PO concept very clear. To call something an overstatement is to accept the basic truth of the statement but signal your reluctance to do so.

5. That PO or something like it is indeed necessary but that it will never work, because we are too conditioned by the YES/NO system.

Answer: Those who agree that we need PO but think that it will not work have the obvious duty to try to make it work instead of backing off in despair.

Four Attitudes

basic function

The general attitudes of PO could be summarized under the following headings:

1. Exploring: Listen, accept other points of view, look for alternatives, look beyond the obvious, do not be satisfied with the adequate.

2. Stimulate: Fantasy, humour, the use of intermediate impossibles and unstable situations as steps to new ideas, try things out, go forward in order to see what happens.

3. Liberate: Introduce discontinuity, escape from concept prisons, escape from old established ideas to better ones, cut through unnecessary complexity, escape from the domination of fixed ideas.

4. Anti-rigidity: Anti-dogmatism, anti-arrogance, against the uniqueness of a particular way of looking at things which excludes all others, challenge fixed ideas, a reminder that the validity of logic cannot go beyond the closed set of concepts to which it is applied.

PO in Action

suggestions

Those who need something more exact than the general attitudes of PO can follow the PO suggestions given below. These are a summary of PO thinking behaviour.

1. Recognize the incompleteness of the YES/NO thinking system. Be aware of its defects, such as rigidity, absolutes, and polarizations, and also of its anti-creative, anti-change nature.
2. Have an understanding of the patterning nature of mind and the consequences of this, in particular the sequence effect and being blocked by openness.
3. Be aware of the danger of continuity in a patterning system and of the concept prisons that make it impossible to look at something in a new way.
4. Understand the significance of humour and the possibility of the insight switch-over to a new way of looking at things.
5. Realize that the PO system is directed towards the perception stage of thinking, in which concepts, attitudes, and values are put together to give the concept package that is then worked upon in the processing stage of thinking.
6. Appreciate that fixed concepts and established ways of looking at things have been set up by a particular sequence of experience and do not have an absolute value.
7. Appreciate that no matter how unique or right an idea may seem it can never exclude other ways of looking at the situation.

8. Accept that even though the current idea may be highly satisfactory other ideas may be just as valid.

9. Make a deliberate effort to generate alternative ways of looking at things instead of just waiting for them.

10. Explore the different ways of looking at things offered by others even if you could not have arrived at them yourself.

11. Know that a conclusion is logically correct only with regard to the starting concept package and that the conclusion has no absolute validity outside this closed system.

12. Accept that another point of view may be perfectly valid even though the conclusion is contrary to your own. It depends on a different starting package.

13. Make an effort to explore and understand the perceptions used by different people who reach different conclusions.

14. Appreciate that an idea may need to be changed later no matter how right it is at the time. Appreciate that you may have to go back and change ideas which were once perfectly correct, in order to move forward to better ideas.

15. Appreciate that an idea is very unlikely to make the best use of available information.

16. Re-examine fixed concepts and assumptions, not because they might be wrong, but because no matter how adequate they are they may be preventing the emergence of better concepts. Appreciate that a worthwhile concept can only be enhanced in value by such a re-examination.

17. Realize that rigidity and dogmatism fossilize ideas and prevent them from evolving into better ideas.

18. Develop and use the PO challenge to uniqueness, rigidity, and dogmatism.

19. Understand that the PO challenge invites an exploration of alternative ideas and is never a judgement to reject the idea challenged – only its uniqueness is rejected.

20. Attack rigidity and dogmatism and exclusive judgements in yourself as much as in others.

21. Prefer the flagpole type of definition to the pigeon-hole-category type.

22. Learn to respond to the PO challenge when it is made against you.

23. Seek to change and improve ideas not by attacking or rejecting them but by using creativity to generate better ones.

24. Instead of being defensive about your ideas be open to new influences as a means of improving your ideas or changing them for better ones.

25. Be more interested in exploring a subject than in proving your point of view or showing how clever you are.

26. Never be afraid to switch to a better idea that comes along, but remember that newness alone does not make an idea better.

27. Saturate the field with ideas when you are trying to solve a problem, and let the most usable one emerge. Be prepared to act upon it. You do not have to wait for the ultimate idea.

28. Learn the specific uses of PO as a creative tool for generating ideas (PO-1, PO-2, PO-3).

29. Understand the use of PO as a discontinuity device to be used for escaping from a situation or way of looking at things which is there only because it was there yesterday.

30. Understand the provocative use of PO to stimulate new ideas.

31. Understand the use of PO for release, escape, cooling it, simplification, and de-escalation.

32. Appreciate that PO is not against continuity but against continuity being sufficient justification for an idea.

33. Understand that the PO system does not seek to effect change by destruction, disruption, clash, confrontation, etc., but by a switch-over to new and better ideas.

34. Understand that what is sought with PO is an insight switch-over from one pattern to a better one and not destruction followed by chaos from which a new pattern is expected to emerge.

35. Understand that PO is a thinking device used to generate new ideas. Before such ideas are acted upon they have to be shown to be better than current ideas. The purpose of PO is to produce new ideas as a basis for change, not to cause change for the sake of it.

36. Appreciate that with PO the readiness to look for a better idea, listen to a better idea, or change to a better idea is what matters most.

37. Note the difference between decisiveness and rigidity. Decisiveness means accepting an idea and acting effectively upon it but being ready to change to a better idea. Rigidity means insisting on the absolute rightness of an idea that will never need changing and then acting upon it.
38. Appreciate that though you yourself may develop your own use of PO, other people may make a different and even fuller use of it.

Three Tools

three systems and three tools

We can place PO by putting it in relation to the basic thinking tools we have and the systems they support:

NO is the basic tool of the logic system.
YES is the basic tool of the belief system.
PO is the basic tool of the creative system.

Together YES and NO give us the traditional YES/NO system. With the addition of PO this becomes the YES/NO/PO system.

PO Experiment

deliberate

PO does work – if you make an effort to use it. Understanding the PO concept in a passive manner is the first step. Deliberate use of PO is the next step. The following experiments illustrate two deliberate uses of PO.

soda siphon

A group of forty-four executives were given a concrete problem to solve. For the first five minutes they exerted their natural creativity. For the next five minutes they used a random word as in PO-2. One of the group suggested a number between 1 and 50 and this indicated a word on a list of fifty ordinary words. The problem was to devise a level indicator for cast-iron soda siphons which tend to run dry as you are in the middle of pouring a drink. The first five minutes produced ideas using a weighing device, a pressure indicator or holes in the sides of the siphon. The random word 'earring' was then introduced and more ideas were produced. All the ideas from the first session and the second session were mixed together and the group voted to choose the idea they liked best. This turned out to be a hollow plastic ball attached by a nylon thread inside the top of the siphon. When the water level was adequate the ball floated but when the level fell below the critical mark the ball hung free and would clang against the side when the siphon was lifted. This preferred idea occurred once before the use of a random word and fourteen times afterwards. In hindsight it is easy to see that the word 'earring' introduced the concept of noise as an indicator and also the concept of something dangling. On another occasion the random word was 'knife' and this time the ideas included a knife edge on the base of the cylinder and an alteration in shape so that a nearly empty cylinder would always tilt slightly over. From the idea of 'cutting the siphon in half' came the notion of two siphons so that you would always have one full.

polarization

The above experiment illustrates the use of PO as a creative tool. The experiment described below shows the use of PO as an attitude. A number of statements were put to different groups: 123 young teachers; 196 science students at university; 78 civil servants; 215 mixed university lecturers and graduates. Each group was divided into two random halves according to whether the birthday date of a person was odd or even.

Statement: 'Capitalism as a system has done more good than harm to society'

	YES/NO	YES/NO/PO
young teachers	45/55	21/17/62
science students	46/54	21/21/58
civil servants	50/50	35/ 5/60
mixed graduates	54/46	22/19/59

The uniformity of response in the YES/NO group is surprising. The addition of the PO opportunity makes a big difference to the numbers agreeing or disagreeing. The most striking difference is in the civil servant group where 50 per cent of the YES/NO group were prepared to disagree with the statement but this was reduced by PO to a mere 5 per cent. In this situation PO provided an apparently needed opportunity to escape polarization and say: 'I accept that as one way of looking at things' (which is how PO was explained to the groups on all occasions).

Statement: 'Democracy is not necessarily the best political system for every country'

	YES/NO	YES/NO/PO
young teachers	89/11	56/18/26
science students	87/13	50/ 4/46
civil servants	78/22	40/15/45
mixed graduates	93/7	48/ 4/48

There is a striking fall in the YES group when the PO opportunity is provided, especially with the mixed graduates (from 93 per cent to 48 per cent). This is all the more surprising when it is pointed out that over 60 per cent of those using YES in the YES/NO group did so with a strong degree of conviction (4 or 5 on a 1 to 5 scale of certainty). This suggests that it is not just the weak and uncertain who take advantage of PO.

Statement: 'Research on the artificial generation of human life should be stopped'

	YES/NO	YES/NO/PO
young teachers	30/70	20/44/36
science students	27/73	20/13/67
civil servants	44/56	30/45/25
mixed graduates	20/80	5/40/55

On this occasion more than 50 per cent of those saying NO used a 4 or 5 degree of conviction. Yet PO still reduced the NO group considerably (from 73 per cent to 13 per cent with the science students). This is especially interesting because science students might have been expected to oppose any restriction on science and yet when given an opportunity to appreciate a different point of view they were happy to do so.

Statement: 'Cannabis is less harmful than alcohol and should be made legal'

	YES/NO	YES/NO/PO
young teachers	55/45	28/33/39
science students	39/61	5/34/61
civil servants	16/84	0/53/47
mixed graduates	52/48	13/28/59

The interesting point with this example is that the YES group was reduced very considerably by PO (from 55 to 28 per cent, from 39 to 5 per cent, from 16 to 0 per cent, from 52 to 13 per cent). This suggests that those who had agreed with the suggestion to legalize cannabis were not really convinced of this but *could not see themselves in the opposite camps*. Thus because their self-image did not allow them to be anti-cannabis they found themselves being pro-cannabis unless they could use PO.

Statement: 'What you can get away with is the basic ethic of modern society'

	YES/NO	YES/NO/PO
young teachers	50/50	31/40/29
science students	40/60	22/39/39
civil servants	42/58	27/42/31
mixed graduates	34/66	19/19/62

Over 50 per cent of those using NO in the YES/NO group used a 4 or 5 degree of certainty and yet this group was reduced by the PO opportunity (e.g. from 73 to 13 per cent and from 80 to 40 per cent). As might be expected the older people in the civil servant group were more inclined than young people to agree with the statement.

What is the significance of these experiments? It seems clear that the PO opportunity is used even by those with apparently strong convictions, so it was not just a let-out for those who were undecided. Other experiments were undertaken to see whether PO served as a rag-bag for the 'don't know' and 'not interested' group. This did not seem to be the case, for when people were allowed to use such responses they still made extensive use of PO.

The purpose of PO in this sort of situation is to provide a by-pass to instant judgement and polarization. Without PO as a defined by-pass people are often forced to make commitments before they are ready to do so. Many people put themselves into one camp on an issue simply because they cannot see themselves (or bear to be seen) in the opposite camp. Once in a camp they adopt the ideas and attitudes of that camp and no longer really think about the situation itself. PO permits a statement to enter the mind in a non-committed way and once inside it can interact with other ideas to produce an eventual decision. Without PO an idea is judged at the gate and labelled YES or NO and thereafter is treated on the emotional basis which such labelling invites.

PO Practice

opportunity

In the animal world, as in the human world, the purpose of play is to try out and develop new skills. The section that follows is a playground for trying out PO. It is not a matter of getting the right answer or getting all the answers. What matters is the effort to look at things in a different way. Even when you are convinced that there can be no other way, you may find a further one in the answer suggestions. The answers are more suggestion than answer because these are open situations and you may come up with answers that are different to those given and perhaps even better ones.

PO Practice

Questions

what you have to do

The following twenty questions are not designed as a test, but unfortunately we are so used to tests that most people will treat them as such. But if it were a test we should be right back with the YES/NO system. Instead the questions are designed as PO exercises. They provide an opportunity to exercise your PO ability. In reading through the book in a passive manner, you may have felt that you understand PO fully. With the following questions you can demonstrate to yourself your understanding of PO and your skill in using it. You may find that passive understanding is not as useful as an active exercise in the use of PO.

difficult

In going through the questions, you will find how difficult it is to change perceptions and to escape from a fixed way of looking at things. You may also find that there is no natural inclination to go beyond the obvious and that you have to make a deliberate effort to do this. Do not be disappointed if you do not seem to be as good at PO as you thought. The questions are not a test of PO ability but more an illustration of PO processes.

no hurry

It is suggested you tackle the questions in groups of four and then look at the answer section for that group. Be careful not to look at the answers or comments to subsequent sections, because you will spoil the exercise for yourself. For each question note down your answer or comments on a piece of paper; otherwise you are likely to suppose that the vague idea you had in your mind was really the same as the actual answer. There is no hurry at all. Speed is not important. You may choose to tackle only one group of questions a day.

genuine effort

Make a genuine effort to tackle the questions. If you simply glance at the question and then immediately look at the answer you will never appreciate PO, for once you have looked at the answer it seems obvious. It is only when you have tried hard to find an answer that you come to realize the need for PO in order to change the way of looking at things.

Group I

1. A suggested solution to the world-population crisis is to allow families to have as many children as they like until they have one boy, and then they must stop having children (voluntary sterilization, etc.). Is this a sensible solution or fair? What effect do you think it would have?
2. Five figures are shown on the right. Pick out the one that is different from all the others.
3. Which ten phenomena in the following list would you regard as being most PO in their effect – that is to say bringing about a change in perceptions as opposed to hardening existing perceptions? The phenomena themselves may actually have been NOPO (rigid and polarized), but the effect may still have been PO.

United Nations	Jumbo Jets
Heart transplantation	The Pentagon
Apollo moon programme	BBC Radio 1
Vietnam	Acupuncture
Women's Lib	Computers
Bangla Desh	The first four-minute mile
The EEC	The Industrial Relations Court
Apartheid	The birth-control pill
The Thalidomide case	Miracle rice
VAT	Hiroshima

4. Which ten people in the following list would you regard as being most PO in their effect? You are not asked to judge the people as being PO or NOPO people, but to judge their effect as events in our society. A PO person might be NOPO in his effect by hardening perceptions, and the other way around.

Picasso	Einstein
General de Gaulle	Marlon Brando
Nixon	Twiggy
Beatles	Lord Longford
Ralph Nader	Enoch Powell
Fidel Castro	Willi Brandt
Freud	Billy Graham
Darwin	Mary Quant
Mao Tse-tung	Mohammed Ali
Pope John	Rudolf Nureyev

(The answer and comment section for the above four questions is on pages 160–61.)

Group II

5. Below are shown eight clusters of four small squares each. In each cluster the squares have been arranged haphazardly. The task is to find some way of dividing the eight clusters into two groups of four. This is done by finding some characteristic which is present in four of the clusters but not in the others.

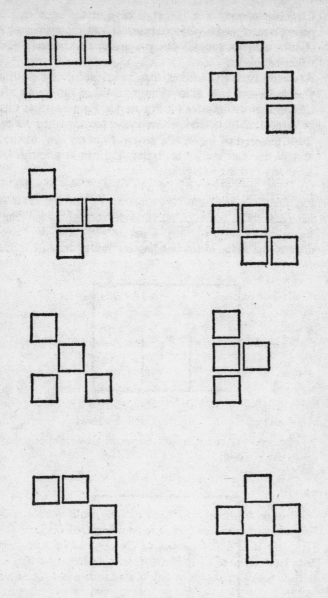

6. Can you conceive of a figure which is at the same time a perfect square and a perfect circle? If you cannot conceive of such a figure yourself can you accept that someone else might be able to?

7. A doctor sincerely believes that by a special test he can predict the sex of a child while it is still in the womb. He charges the parents a fee for this service. But he accepts that he is not infallible, and whenever he proves wrong he returns the original fee with a generous ten per cent interest as well. He makes a lot of money. Then he is arrested. Of what do you think he is guilty?

8. (a) Below are shown two different views of the same building. One is a bird's-eye view from above, and the other is from directly on front (i.e. plan and elevation of the building, to use an architect's terms). What do you think the three-dimensional shape of the building is? Try to draw it.

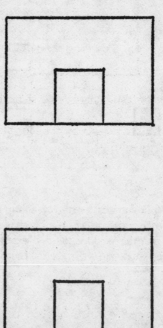

(b) Below are shown two different views of the same object. In the first the object is viewed directly from in front. In the second the object is viewed directly from the side. What

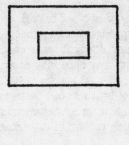

do you think the three-dimensional shape of the object is? Try to draw it.

(The answers and comments on the four questions in Group II are given on pages 162–4.)

Group III

9. Each of the following is a way of doing things which we have developed in our society. Although these ways may be adequate, it may be possible to find alternatives. Can you begin to think of alternatives to each of them?

exams in schools and colleges
advertising
prisons
hospitals

newspapers
two-party democracy
buses for public transport
insurance

10. A design is shown below. The task is to break down this design into component parts so that you could describe it simply. How many different ways of looking at the design can you find? Each way must involve some different principle of organization.

11. A pollution-patrol boat sets out on its usual journey, which takes it upstream and then downstream and finally upstream again to its starting point. On this occasion the river is run-

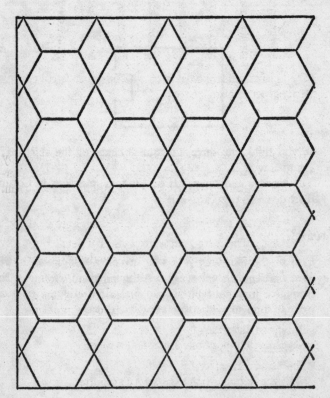

ning faster than usual. Will this make any difference to the time taken over the whole journey?

12. Eight black strips are shown below, and the problem is to convert them into seven black strips which are equal in length without losing any of the black material. The obvious way would be to chop one strip into seven sections and add one section to each of the remaining strips. Can you think of another way of doing it?

(The answers and comments on the four questions in Group III are given on pages 164–9.)

Group IV

13. Two problems are given below. Each problem is followed by an intermediate impossible. Make deliberate use of the intermediate impossible to arrive at an approach to the problem.

   Problem: Poverty.
   Intermediate impossible: PO money should grow on trees.

   Problem: The next improvement in TV sets.
   Intermediate impossible: PO they should be good to eat.

14. Two problems are given below. Each problem is followed by a random juxtaposition. Make deliberate use of the random juxtaposition to arrive at an approach to the problem.

   Problem: Inflation.
   Random juxtaposition: Inflation PO shoes.

   Problem: Car safety.
   Random juxtaposition: Car safety PO butter.

15. A podle is a doodle which can be interpreted in a variety of different ways. The podle is drawn first and then you try to discover all the different things it could represent, making an effort to find as many as possible. Three separate podles are shown below. For each one write down as many different interpretations as you can.

16. Humour and PO are closely linked. A deliberate humour situation can be provoked by putting together a well-known

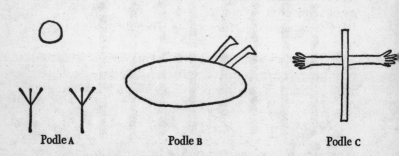

Podle A   Podle B   Podle C

person and a random word and then seeing how quickly the two can be connected up. I often do this in my lectures. On one occasion the well-known person was Mr Wilson and the random word suggested by the audience was 'mushroom' (suggested without any knowledge of the person involved).

PO Mr Wilson is a mushroom.

How might you snap the two concepts together?

(The answers and comments on the four questions in Group IV are given on pages 170–4.)

Group V

17. Below are given two apparently extraordinary situations. The task is to use your imagination to construct a scenario which would explain these situations and make them appear quite reasonable. For each situation generate as many different explanations as you can.

A man is standing by his car pouring beer into his petrol tank.

All the senior executives are standing by as the big safe is carefully opened. When the door finally swings open it reveals a black velvet cushion on top of which rests a solitary peanut.

18. Show with a drawing how you would redesign the human head if God were to ask you to do this for him.

19. Can you think immediately of two people in your life whom you would consider PO people? And two people whom you would consider NO PO people?

    Do the same thing for people in public life (politics, art, sport, etc.).

20. When shapes are symmetrical it is easy to divide them into two equal halves, because you can see at once where the dividing line should go. But the two shapes shown below are not .

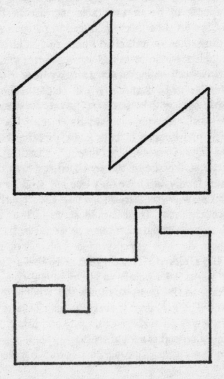

symmetrical. Nevertheless each shape can be divided into two exactly equal halves (equal in shape, area, etc.). How would you draw the line that divides each shape into two such identical halves?

(The answers and comments on questions in Group V are given on pages 174-6.)

Answers and Comments

Answers to Group I Questions

1. This would seem to be a silly suggestion at first. No family would have more than one boy, but some families would have two, three, four, five, or even more girls. Thus there would appear to be an inevitable increase in the ratio of girls to boys. In time this would lead to polygamy, and since a man can father an unlimited number of children the population problem would be as bad as ever. But if you go beyond this obvious way of looking at things you will find that an equal number of boys and girls will be born. This is because the female eggs will be fertilized just as they are now, and since no fertilized eggs are actually rejected they must end up as an equal number of boys and girls being born. Even if fertilized eggs were rejected through abortion this would not matter if the sex of the fertilized egg was not known. Since each family can have only one boy, and an equal number of girls are born, then on average each family can have only two children. These would serve just to replace the parents, and the population increase would be halted. (There would be a decrease actually, since not everyone gets married or has children.) The suggestion is also a good one because it allows each family to go on having children until a son is born, and in many countries this birth of a son is very important. The PO effect is that you may have to go beyond the obvious way of looking at things to find that an apparently silly suggestion makes a lot of sense.

2. Sixty-three per cent of people choose the triangle as the odd

man out because it is the only figure with no curves in it. If you chose this you are right. But you are also right if you chose any one of the others. Each figure can be considered the odd man out if you choose to look at the figures in different ways:

1st: the only one with more than two axes of symmetry.
2nd: the only one with no curves.
3rd: the only one with no axes of symmetry.
4th: the only one with both a curve and a straight line.
5th: the only one which would fall over if solid.

So your being right does not stop other people from being right as well. Furthermore, if you make an effort to look at things in different ways you can come up with different answers. Both of these are the PO points for this question. Unfortunately in education we are trained to stop looking for other answers as soon as we have found the first one.

3. There are no right or wrong answers. What mattered was the exercise of your judgement in considering which phenomena were most PO in quality. Someone else may pick out a completely different lot from the list. You are both right, because your choice depends on the way you choose to look at things. You may look at the Pentagon as having a PO effect because it has changed people's perceptions about war, but someone else may look at it as an example of rigid NOPO attitudes. You should be able to discuss the reasons behind each of your choices with someone else. It is valuable to compare choices in this way so that you can develop your understanding of PO.

4. The comments that applied to the previous question apply to this one as well. Again there are no right and wrong answers. This question is more difficult than the previous one because you have to separate the characteristics of a person from his effect on society. With both these questions the PO effect is to appreciate different ways of looking at things and also to exercise your own understanding of PO while you use it as a basis for a judgement.

Answers to Group II Questions

5. The traditional analytical approach is to examine the clusters to see what existing features can be used for the discrimination: edges in contact, free corners, axes of symmetry, orientation, etc. You may have made your discrimination on this basis and your answer will be right. But if you adopt a different approach and see *what can be done* with the clusters, then you may find that four of the clusters can be made into a compact square by moving just one small square in each case. This is shown opposite. The PO effect here is to break away from the usual static approach which examines what is to see *what can be done*.

6. You would be right to insist that there is an absolute logical contradiction in a figure that is at the same time a perfect square and a perfect circle. And yet it is possible for someone to perceive such a figure. I have given people the suggestion that when they awoke from a hypnotic trance they would see on the wall in front of them a figure which was at the same time a perfect square and a perfect circle. This figure would appear when I gave a certain signal word. About an hour later I would give this signal word and the person would suddenly concentrate on the wall in front of him and would try to describe what he saw. He would get quite frantic as he maintained that it was a circle but had corners but was really round and yet a square. He would grab a pencil and try to draw the shape but would immediately scratch out each line as it was drawn. This *experience* of a square circle does not mean that such a shape can logically exist, but simply that the perception of the shape can exist. The PO effect is whether you are prepared to accept a perception that runs counter to logic or a perception that you yourself cannot conceive.

7. You may have found this question easy. But is it easy if you look at it again? Instinctively you feel that the doctor is guilty, but of what is he guilty? He himself sincerely believes in his method. When he is right the parents are happy and consider the money well spent. When he is wrong

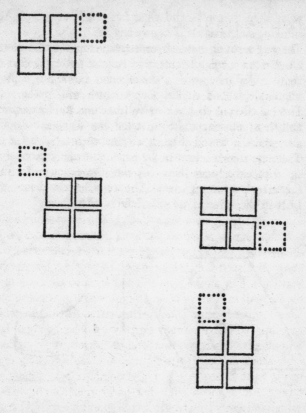

he apologizes, points out that he never claimed infallibility, and not only returns the money but adds a generous interest to it. So of what is he guilty:

Of making money?
Of not doing statistics?
Of believing in something he had not proved?
Of not giving his clients an accurate estimate of error?
Of offering a service of which others disapprove?

Clearly the doctor would make money even if his test was useless. But in society a lot of people are allowed to sell what they believe in and what has not been proved. Your thinking on the matter is its own answer.

8. There is a strong natural tendency to suppose that both of the shapes are cubical. This is because only straight lines and right angles are shown in the different views. But it proves impossible to find cubical shapes which will fit the views. The PO effect is to break away from this fixed expectation and then you may realize that the first shape is a diagonal slice and the second shape is a drum with a notch cut out. These are shown below. In my experience many people come up with cube suggestions, but these have not so far fitted the actual drawings given. The conventions about using lines in the different views are the standard ones.

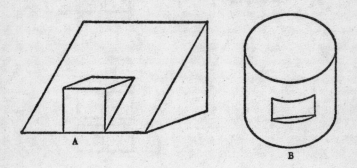

A

B

Answers to Group III Questions

9. It is unlikely that you would have been able to find alternatives better than the existing ways of doing things that were listed. This is because the time at your disposal would have been limited. But what matters is the attitude involved, that is to say your *willingness* to look afresh at something that is taken for granted. Did you try for an alternative in each case? Did you come up with some sort of alternative? Or did you regard the question as silly and turn to the answer section?

10. Different ways of looking at and breaking down the given design are shown below.

    (a) Columns of hexagons are built up and then slid towards each other until they touch.

(b) Strings of diamond shapes hang down from above. They are parallel but separated from each other. Cross links join the lateral apices of the diamond shapes.

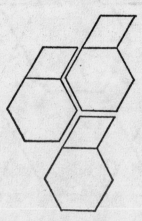

(c) The basic unit is a hexagon with a small parallelogram stuck on its upper edge. These basic units, all orientated in the same direction, are fitted together as closely as possible, leaving no gaps.

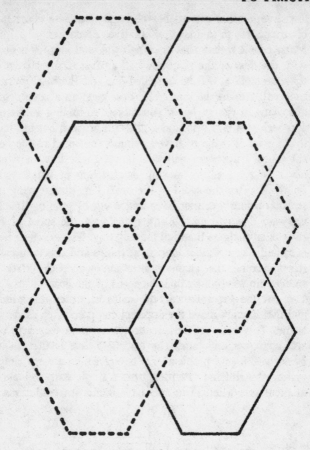

(d) There are two overlying designs. Each is made up of flattened hexagons which mesh with each other as in chicken coop wire. The two identical designs are then laid one over the other.

You may have come up with other ways of looking at the design than those given above. If your suggestions work, then they are also right. The PO effect is to show how different approaches can all be valid and that with effort it is often possible to find such alternative approaches.

11. Many people reckon that since half the total journey is made with the flow of the river and half against it any change in the rate of flow will be cancelled out and the total journey time will remain the same. This does seem an adequate way of looking at things, but if you succeed in finding a different approach you will also find a different answer. For instance, if the river is made to flow at almost the speed of the boat the journey upstream will take hours. These lost hours can never be regained by moving downstream at what would be about twice the speed of the boat. Time lost moving upstream obviously cannot be cancelled out by gaining time on the way downstream. So any increase in the speed of the river must increase the total journey time. The PO effect here is to find a new way of looking at things and also to use as a stepping-stone the changed situation where the river is speeded up to almost equal the speed of the boat.

12. You cut the paper bearing the strips in a stepwise fashion and then simply move the upper piece up one step as shown below. This automatically reduces the pieces to seven and also elongates each one. The PO effect here is that an apparently difficult problem can be solved in a very simple manner by shifting attention from a single strip to looking at them as a whole. You may have found other solutions.

Answers to Group IV Questions

13. You should have been able to generate an approach to the problem from the intermediate impossible in each case. The ideas you obtained may be very different from those given below. These are simply examples of what might have happened:

Poverty: Fruit grows on trees, but you still have to pick it. There are people who grow fruit trees and those who pick the fruit. Poor people are often so disadvantaged in terms of education that they cannot compete directly for employment. So perhaps we could create a new profession which would function like the fruit growers to package and process work opportunities. Such people would be paid directly by the government a direct percentage of the wages earned.

TV sets' improvement: You eat when you are hungry, and when you are not hungry you store the food in cupboards or the refrigerator. But with TV at the moment you have to take the programmes when they are offered whether you are hungry or not. So the next improvement will be a recording system and a pre-set time switch so that you can record programmes while you are asleep or at the office and then play them back exactly when you want them. This would allow more specialized programmes.

14. As with the previous question, you should have been able to use the random juxtaposition to generate ideas of your own. The ones given below are no more than examples of what might have happened.

Inflation: You always have two shoes which are very similar but not exactly the same. Your right shoe is for your right foot and your left shoe for your left foot. So perhaps there could be two currency values: one for buying and one for paying people. The paying rate would remain standard and the buying rate would be adjusted periodically by the government. Thus wages would be paid in standard pounds, but when used in stores as a buying currency the pound might be worth 110p one week and 120p another week, according to the need to adjust the economy. Actual wage rates would not need changing so much, since purchasing power would keep pace with any rise in the cost of living. A simple conversion machine by the cash register would convert marked price on the goods into buying price that week.

Car safety: From the dashboard protrude padded mushrooms on stalks. The stalks end in perforated discs which move backwards and forwards inside sealed cylinders filled with a buttery substance. A switch allows this substance to be heated and as it goes fluid the mushroom head is adjusted to fit the passenger. When the heat is turned off, the substance, like butter, goes harder and provides a viscous resistance to movement of the mushroom. On impact the disc is forced through the viscous material, so providing a deceleration less abrupt than with a seat belt.

15. Suggested interpretations of all three podles are given below. Some of them may appear pretty wild. You yourself may have come up with some of the suggestions listed or you may have ones that are completely different. The PO effect is to realize that even when you seem to have run out of new ideas there are always others you have not yet thought of.

PODLE A

Two TV aerials and the sun
Man with two artificial hands learning to throw a ball
Frayed ends of broken rope falling off a pulley
Tattoo design for navel and thighs
Hieroglyphics
Psychiatric test for astronauts
Tramps' sign language
Bird waiting for worm to emerge from hole
Hen examining the first egg she has laid
Flowers opening in the sunlight
Two trees and the moon
Bombs dropping from a rocket
Multiple re-entry nuclear rocket (MIRV)
Ball game with goalposts

Girl wearing flippers on beach and talking to a man who is
    standing on his head to impress her
Bird prints
Two broken tennis rackets and a ball
Two spacecraft travelling from a planet
Several months after a frightened ostrich standing on a patch
    of wet concrete tried to bury its head
Upside-down view of braces and a navel
A bird learning to play soccer
Bird flying over tennis court killed by tennis ball

PODLE B

Diving into water
Monster emerging from lake
Hovercraft
Spacecraft
Personal flying saucer
Mexican having a siesta
Two giraffes appearing through ground mist
Overturned surfboard
Upside-down view of parachute enveloping instructor
Suction-type clothes-peg hanger
Ambitious French baker overwhelmed
Upside-down view of 'man under a cloud'
Upside-down view of 'man with his head in the clouds'
Man carrying out repairs to a boat
Modern sculptor whose work has collapsed on him
Upside-down view of Boy Scout trying to erect a tent
Submarine with snorkel
Timid warrior whose shield is too big for him
Mating dinosaurs behind a rock
Upside-down view of 98-leg-amputee centipede
Bread roll stabbed in the back (twice)
Snail that has lost its shell
Upside-down view of discus thrower just before discus hits
    you
Upside-down view of angel slipping through a cloud

PODLE C

A man with his head trapped in a door
A matchstick man with big arms hiding behind a matchstick
Pair of rubber gloves in the middle of a road
A friendly waving cross
Frozen rubber gloves on a washline
Christ without crossbar
Tree reflected in water
Totem pole
Welcome-home sign
One hand in a mirror
Part of a puppet
Weather vane
Plaster casts for making rubber gloves
Special clapping apparatus for audience in TV show
Artificial arms for pickpocket to keep in view while his own
    do the picking
Man trying to escape from closed elevator
New design for men – to economize on world food scarcity
Scarecrows
Automated traffic policeman stopping all traffic
Beggar coming around corner past plate-glass window
Starved fisherman showing size of ones that got away
Symbol of the Friendship Party
Stick used by architects for measuring width of doors
Intermediate handshake device for politicians who do not
    actually want to touch each other
Sideways view of arm emerging from lake to grab the Sword
    Excalibur
Last glimpse of drowning man (plus reflection)
Double back-scratcher for two group-therapy people standing
    back to back
Jeweller's display stand for rings
Pair of gloves drying on a stand
Device for teaching seamen semaphore
Avant-garde version of a crucifix

16. Your satisfaction with your own version is your answer. On the occasion in question the following comments were offered:

'Functions best when kept in the dark and fed on rubbish.'

'A shilling for a pound.'

'The centre of a ring of fairies.'

'Can be poisonous at times.'

'All head and no substance.'

'Expensive.'

'Easily trodden on but keeps coming back again.'

Answers to Group V Questions

17. Below are some suggested explanations of the two extraordinary situations offered. You yourself will have different explanations. The explanations should be as reasonable as possible. The PO effect here is to look at the situation in as many different ways as possible in order to see what may have led up to it.

Beer into petrol tank:

He was trying to establish that he was drunk as an alibi for a crime he was about to commit.

There was a false bottom in the petrol tank, and a refugee was hidden in this compartment. The beer was for the refugee.

He was trying out a secret new petrol which was disguised as beer so rivals would not notice it.

A simple-minded fellow who had heard that alcohol was added to petrol for racing cars to improve their performance.

He was demonstrating a new engine which did not have a carburettor. Jets of air were forced through the petrol tank, carrying petrol vapour into the engine. In this arrangement the addition of beer would not matter, since only the petrol vapour entered the engine.

Peanut in the safe:

A master burglar had got there first and had replaced the largest diamond in the world with a peanut.

A hypnotist had hypnotized them all as he sold them a peanut as the largest diamond in the world.

A very wealthy man had died and indicated in his will that his special safe was to be opened in the presence of the executives of his company and the contents given to his children. The peanut was his eccentric way of indicating that wealth was valueless.

A riddle left by a wealthy man who directed that his fortune should be left to whichever of his children could solve the riddle of the peanut.

A special secret code signal.

An exceptional mutation of peanut which was capable of giving a special taste not obtained with any other peanut.

Failure of an experiment in which a peanut completely isolated from the possibility of fraud was going to be changed into gold by special rays.

The safe contains very advanced electronic equipment for de-materializing matter which is then sent through space and reassembled. The peanut in the safe has just been sent back in this way by astronauts in outer space.

A very special type of lock which is operated by computer recognition of a unique shape. The peanut is the unique shape the computer has learned to recognize. If the peanut is lost the bank vaults cannot be opened.

18. When asked to redesign the human head, most people suggest extra eyes, eyes on top of the head, or eyes at the back of the head. Another popular suggestion is for earlids to close down our ears when we wanted silence. It is difficult to come up with a really new design, because we are so satisfied with our heads as they are. The PO effect here is to come up with a new idea. The important point is whether or not you come up with a design and how difficult you find it.

19. Did you have any difficulty in coming up with the eight names required? Were the NOPO names easier than the PO

ones or the other way around? Was the difficulty that you were not really sure about the classifications or in finding people to fit them?

20. At first it may seem rather difficult to divide the shapes into half. But if you make a PO jump and start by *doubling* the shapes it becomes very easy. Each shape can be doubled into a square. You now repeat at right angles to itself the line that is dividing the square in half. The square is thus divided into quarters. Two of the quarters provide the two halves of the original shape in each case. The process is shown below.

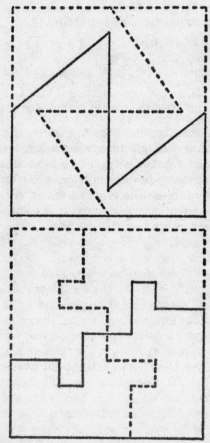

Conclusion

PO *quotient* (PQ)

IQ tests work on the YES/NO basis, for there are right answers which you have to get. But your PO is not measured by your actual success in tackling the twenty questions. PQ does not depend on getting pre-set right answers or even any answers at all. PQ is a rating of your understanding of PO and your willingness to use it.

There are three stages in acquiring PO ability:

1. An understanding of the nature of PO and an acceptance of the need to change perceptions.
2. A willingness to try to generate new perceptions and a willingness to accept different ways of looking at things.
3. An actual skill in using PO as an attitude and as a tool.

Acquiring skill for the third stage is a matter of practice and confidence, and it does take time. But the first two stages are really much more important. So your PQ is based on your willingness to look at things in different ways rather than on your success. That is why you rate your own PQ, because no one else can measure for you your willingness to look at things in different ways and to escape from rigid patterns.